graveyard

*girl*

# graveyard girl

*(stories)*

wendy a. lewis

RED DEER
PRESS

RED DEER PRESS
Box 5005
56 Avenue & 32 Street
Red Deer Alberta Canada T4N 5H5

*Acknowledgments*
Edited by Peter Carver
Cover photo by FPG International
Cover and book design by Duncan Campbell
Printed and bound in Canada by Friesens for Red Deer Press

The biblical quotations in "Revelations" are from the King James Version, published by Thomas Nelson Publishers, Nashville © 1984.

Financial support provided by the Canada Council, the Department of Canadian Heritage and the Alberta Foundation for the Arts, a beneficiary of the Lottery Fund of the Government of Canada.

Canadian Cataloguing in Publication Data

Lewis, Wendy A., 1966-
Graveyard girl: stories

ISBN 0-88995-202-7

I. Title
PS8573.E9913G72 2000      jC813'.6      C00-910200-0
PZ7.L588Gr 2000

5 4 3 2 1

*For Mom, who has stirred the waters all my life,*
*and for Peter, who unlocked the floodgates*

# contents

## acknowledgments

The first drafts of these stories came swiftly, following the birth of my first daughter. How proud I was of myself until I showed them to my writing workshop and discovered how awful they were—messy as afterbirth! But at least they were born. They were just young and had a long way to grow, like premature babies.

To all the people who helped me raise them, my deepest heartfelt thanks. To Peter Carver, Kathy Stinson and all my writing workshop friends (special thanks to Loris Lesynski, Rick Book, Anne Carter, Lena Coakley and Hadley Dyer); to Mom, who patiently read each draft and donated countless hours of baby-sitting; to the wonderful staff at Stonemoor Day Care Center; to my friends and family who over the years have shared their anecdotes, jokes and sayings, some of which found their way onto these pages; to the experts-in-their-fields who wisely advised me: Dad, Agnes Mitchell, Anna MacKay-Smith, Kenneth Welsh, Rita Tindlay, Rick Book, Kelly (the "Vice") Boehm, Rob Murray, Reverend Andrew Allison and Dr. Terry Bryon; to other people who helped me enormously (but have no idea they've done it) by writing books or giving talks that inspired and motivated me to keep writing—Sarah Ellis, Tim Wynne-Jones, Brian Doyle, Noel Baker, Karen Hesse and Professor David Blostein. And finally, a great big thank-you to Rob, Amelia and Maddy for supporting me, encouraging me and loving me in spite of everything.

# prologue

# (Ginger)

Call me crazy, but I heard whispering. The kind of whispering kids do, low enough so you can't hear the details, loud enough so it gets on your nerves.

It was coming from the top shelf of the wall unit, where I never remember to dust. At first I thought Ray must've put the tape player up there for a joke. He pulls stunts like that sometimes, practical jokes that backfire and scare the wits out of me, like the time in bed when he wore a stocking over his head and turned on a flashlight under his chin. When your husband does stuff like that, you get to expect it, so I shovelled off the ottoman (Ray's chip 'n' dip station during hockey season play-offs,) and hauled myself up.

I was wrong about the tape player, but right about the dust, which seemed to lie like fog over junk I forgot we had. Like the Buddha statue with the clock in his belly, which someone gave us for a wedding present, and the teapot Lil made for me in the Moms 'n' Daughters ceramic class I wouldn't to go to 'cause I wasn't her real daughter, and some little toys I must have put up high so Jo wouldn't choke on them. That tells you how long it's been since I looked on the top shelf. Jo's seven now, and hasn't been eating toys for quite some time!

A few books were up there, too, the kind you want to keep but don't want to look at all the time. Like Lil's mama's Bible. A book of poems from high school. And my yearbook from 1982.

I stared at the spine of that yearbook so long my bare feet stuck to the naugahyde ottoman. Stared 'cause that's where the voices were coming from. Had the feeling that if I opened it, I'd get sucked in and chewed up, till there was nothing left for Ray to come home to but my sweaty footprints on the naughahyde.

I opened it anyway. Real casual, like I was just gonna flip through. But it fell open to the page I must've stared at a million times back then. Fell open and laid there, the picture staring up at me, as if it was remembering, too . . .


Man, the voices.

The faces.

The picture's in full color, bright as ever. I thought pictures were supposed to fade with time, but not this one.

There's Tish looking like she'd rather be someplace else. Dress makes her look more like a cupcake than a bridesmaid. Wonder why she did it? Tish hates that stuff—dresses, makeup, high heels. Fairy tales . . .

Mandy Solesby looks thrilled to be the other bridesmaid, though. If she grinned any wider, her face'd split in half like a muppet's. She had dimples coming out her rear end, that one, sweet as a butter tart . . .

Who's Alex Meyers supposed to be in that tacky yellow dress? Oh yeah. Princess Anne. I guess that was the style back then. Back when Tish and Alex were still best friends. Back when Alex was still alive. Man . . .

Kate Kernohan got to be the queen, surprise, surprise. When

you're already Student Council president and captain of the cheerleading team, why stop there?

Miss Twitchit of course was the Queen Mum, looking soft and frothy as toothpaste spit in her mint green dress. Good disguise! The Twitchit I remember had hair permed so tight, it looked like a bathing cap covered with shiny grey marbles. And a hand-knit Union Jack sweater with a row of souvenir spoons pinned like medals to her chest. I can still hear her voice blasting through the megaphone like a space shuttle take-off, full of smelly hot air. Demanding our undivided attention! Reminding us what a privilege it was to help recreate the Wedding of the Century! As if we had a choice . . .

I can hardly see Naylor Whitehead behind all the frills and flounces, but certain features stand out, so to speak. Those ears! And that Adam's apple! Poor guy, looks like he swallowed a golf ball. Who was Naylor supposed to be? Oh yeah, Prince Edward.

And Jewel's boyfriend, Jake, was Prince Andrew. Teeth as big and white as bathroom tiles, but most people thought he was good-looking. He really could pass for Prince Andrew, if you squinted a bit and looked at him sideways . . .

Jewel looks every inch the princess in that god-damned wedding dress it took sixty of us the whole year to make in Family Studies class. On the day of the wedding, she dumped grape juice down the front, and all she worried about was looking bad for the pictures. God, I hated her. Her and those kids she brought from the day care to be flower girls and page boys. Stuck to her like spit bugs on a long-legged weed. As if she didn't already have enough people putting her on a pedestal, she had to recruit her own hero worshippers . . .

Beside Jewel's is the face I've been avoiding. Might as well try not looking at the moon when it rises up full and huge and shining like the sun. Derek Papp. Hockey star and one-time boyfriend of yours truly. Doesn't look much like Prince Charles, but he sure looks like a Prince Charming, dammit. . . . God, just once I wish I could look at his face without feeling like I'm having a heart attack.

Who's he smiling at, off to the side? Not me, that's for sure. I was straight ahead. Not in the picture, but taking it. Helping out the town photographer. You don't go to the trouble of staging a show like this and trust the job to the high school Camera Club. No sir. But he let me press the shutter release. Felt like I was pulling a trigger.

There's a smell rising off these pages like steam from a bath. A smell that grabs me by the eyeballs, and pulls me back in time. The smell of me, back then. The smell of Loves' Baby Soft bubble bath with the pink bottle and white round lid. I used to sit in the tub with this yearbook propped on my knees, sweat and bath water dripping down my nose. Must've been the bath water that crinkled the page so bad. That, or tears.

Can almost hear Lil, rapping on the bathroom door, asking if I'm okay. And that free-loader Albert, whining in the background about me wasting water. "How dirty can she get?" he'd mutter. As if he didn't know.

Above the wedding picture is a fingerprint. I put my fingers over it, one at a time, looking for a match. Thumbkin, Pointer, Tall Man, Ring Man, Pinky. Jo's favorite song when she still liked Barney. Sometimes, I catch myself humming the tune. "Where is Thumbkin? Where is Thumbkin?" When you think about it, it's pretty weird to lose part of yourself, but I understand how it happens. Some days, I look at the stranger in the mirror and wonder: "Where is Ginger? Where is Ginger?"

My pinky finger matches the fingerprint. I guess weight gain doesn't affect fingertips, but farther up, fat bulges around the ring I dug out of my jewellery box this morning. A gold figure eight with two diamond chips. Figure eight for eternity. What a joke! Used to call it a promise ring and wear it on the fourth finger of my left hand, but it doesn't fit now that I'm eighteen years older and eighty pounds heavier and besides, my wedding band is there. So, I've got it on my pinky finger and even that pinches, but I leave it on. This morning, I want to remember the hurt.

Jo's up, banging around the kitchen. Soon she'll come looking for me. Mustn't let her catch me tearing up a book. One quick rip, the page is out. I fold it together with the clipping I cut from this morning's paper, and stuff them both into my pocket just as Jo bursts into the room, singing Happy Birthday.

What a doll. She's brought me a muffin with a birthday candle in it. She must've used my cigarette lighter from the top of the fridge, and I'm tempted to tell her off. Fire's dangerous, I'm about to say. But then, so is looking in old yearbooks.

Instead, I give her a hug, and make a wish before blowing out the candle.

What I wish for is—well, I can't say what it is or it won't come true. But one thing's for damn sure. I'm gonna make the wish come true today.

1983

# (Mandy)

I love this book Dad gave me. I love the lilies on its cover and the Greek symbols hand painted on their petals. I love not knowing what they mean, but knowing that someday I might find out. I love the way it creaks when I open it because no one besides me has opened it before. I love the new smell of its pages, with nothing on them but a small grey scroll in each corner.

I've never had such a beautiful book. It's the kind of book you save for sacred thoughts or inspirations, like the ones John had in the Book of Revelation. *Write the things which thou hast seen, and the things which are, and the things which shall be hereafter.* That's what Jesus told him.

I wonder if that's what Dad was thinking when he gave me the book last night. We'd been packing for our annual trek to Dorey Lake. Our first family reunion without Mom.

We tried to keep everything the same. We made Mom's potato salad, and her brownies with the cream cheese frosting. We packed a picnic lunch to eat in the car so we wouldn't have to stop. Mom always hated to stop.

But some things can't be the same. I'm not squished in the back seat with the cooler, free to stare out the window and daydream. I'm sitting up front in Mom's place, and there's all this wide open space between Dad and me with no words to fill it up.

The book gives me an excuse not to talk, but I don't know what to write. I think Dad wants me to write about Mom, and I guess I should. But I don't know where to start and besides, it's not Mom's face I see staring up at me from the page. It's Eden's.

Aunt Christy nearly came through the phone yesterday when she told us her darling wayward Eden would be at the reunion, her first in four years. I've been filled with dread ever since. She'll be there in stiletto heels and something slinky, sipping wine from a glass rimmed with red lipstick smiles. Or maybe she'll be in costume, wearing a baggy dress and Birkenstocks and sipping Aunt Christy's herbal tea from a china cup. Either way, she'll hand out hugs and kisses and compliments and everyone will forgive her. Then she'll tell them her story. She'll tell them where she saw me that night in Toronto, and then I'll die. Or have to find a new family. A new father. Of course she'll tell, why wouldn't she? Eden has nothing to lose, and I have everything.

*In the beginning, there was Eden.*

After the darkness came light, and I knew that the light was good. I woke in a garden filled with heady perfumes and luscious fruits and a sun shining overhead, a sun that smiled and said my name, *Mandy.*

Mom said newborn babies can't remember things like that. She said there was no way I could remember the flowers and fruit baskets that filled the hospital room, or that my four-year-old cousin Eden held me and said my name, but I do remember. I remember smiling my first smile at her, then breaking into a wail. Because even in the beginning, I loved Eden, but I was afraid of her, too.

I remember playacting in her room, in secret because our parents wouldn't like it. She let me play the choice parts of Cinderella or Snow White or Little Red Riding Hood, and she'd be the wicked stepmother or the evil queen or the wolf. She was a good actress. She really made me believe I was in danger. Sometimes I could see murder in her eyes. We acted out Bible stories, too. I played Abel and she played Cain, sneaking up behind me and closing murderous fingers around my throat. After, she'd hug and kiss me like nothing had happened, but I always felt exhausted after one of those secret plays, as if I'd been killed and brought back to life.

Before we went back downstairs, she'd brush out my hair in front of her mirror and tell me that since our fathers were brothers, and both ministers, too, we were the closest thing to being sisters. The sound of her voice and the feel of her fingers in my hair sent me into a lovely hypnotic trance and I'd believe anything she said then.

When Eden was eight, she decided she had better things to do than hang around with a pesky little cousin. First chance she'd get, she'd drop whatever we were doing to run off and play with her older friends. I'd spend the rest of the visit curled on Dad's lap, sucking my thumb.

One day, though, I remember having Eden all to myself. She was twelve and I was eight. We were sitting by the little stream behind their house. I loved that stream with its darting minnows and dragonflies, and interesting bits of trash that got caught along the shore, but Eden kept sighing with boredom. She started pointing out stuff on the opposite shore that belonged to the park. Teenagers would go there at night and leave behind cigarette butts and beer bottles and, that day, a used condom, long, sheer, and iridescent. Eden told me what it was for. I didn't believe her. I said it was a balloon, and she laughed at me. "Oh Mandy, you're such an innocent."

We threw sticks in the water to watch them tumble downstream. Mine kept getting caught in the tangle of weeds and trash, while Eden's sailed straight ahead and disappeared around the bend.

"Someday, that'll be me, taking off for adventure," said Eden. "And you'll be stuck at home, poor little Mandy, too scared to ever leave." Then she told me they really were leaving. Her family was moving up north to Dorey Lake, and I'd only see her once a year, at reunion time.

I knew I was an ugly duckling. I didn't need Eden to tell me that, although she did, several times. The year I turned twelve, I had braces, glasses, hair that wouldn't curl and I slouched my shoulders to hide the fact that I'd "blossomed early," as Mom put it.

Four times we'd made the trek to Dorey Lake. Eden was sixteen that year, and beautiful. For two days she ignored me and flirted with the older boy cousins who couldn't keep their eyes off her. I didn't mind. I helped in the kitchen, read to my Great Aunt Ethel, and went for walks along the lakefront. Then Mom and Dad decided to stay a few days longer. I dreaded the other cousins leaving, and being alone with Eden all day.

But when the others left, she became a different person, more like the Eden I worshipped as a kid. She sat me down in front of her mirror and gently pulled my shoulders back. "Show them off!" she whispered. Giggling, she brushed out my hair. It was years since anyone but me had brushed my hair, but it had the same hypnotic effect as it did before. She put some color on my cheeks and lips. I never wore makeup. Mom didn't approve of it. But I liked it. I didn't look like an ugly duckling anymore. I smiled at Eden in the mirror.

"Those train tracks'll be off before you know it," she said. "Then you'll have a beautiful smile."

The next day she took me to her secret place. We hiked a mile or so through the bush until she stopped and asked what I saw.

"Trees?" I said, feeling stupid. I didn't notice anything different. It was a beautiful spot, but so were all the forests around Dorey Lake.

"What kind of trees?" she asked.

"I don't know . . . pine, spruce . . ." I didn't know the names of all the young trees growing between the thick trunks of the older trees. Then I saw above me, the hint of round, green fruit, hidden in the leaves.

"Apple trees!" I said. "How did they get here?"

"Dad says there was a house here a long time ago," said Eden. "This must've been the orchard. I come here to get away, when my folks are driving me crazy."

"I know what you mean," I said. "There's a willow tree at home that I climb when I need to be alone."

"Don't tell me you have parent problems, too?"

"Well . . . not exactly."

Eden reached into a hole in the trunk of an apple tree and took out an old cookie tin. She pried off the lid and pulled out some cigarettes and matches.

She offered me one but I shook my head. I wondered if she'd gone crazy. Her parents hated smoking. No one was allowed to smoke in their house. Her dad would smell it on us a mile away.

Still, I admired her guts. She took a long, deep drag of the cigarette. The tip of it glowed. I wondered what it felt like to have smoke inside you. *Lead us not into temptation,* I thought.

"I'll tell you a secret," she said. "I'm thinking of leaving home."

"Running away?"

She nodded.

"But why, Eden?"

"The question is, why *not?* My life is *unbearable.* You have *no* idea. Mom and Dad watch every move I make, and even when I'm out of their sight, God's watching, or so Dad says." She laughed.

"My Omniscient Jailer. I bet He's watching right now and writing in His little book, *Mandy's a good girl. She turned down the cigarette.* You're a chosen one, Mandy! A lamb. You probably shouldn't be talking to me. I'm one of the Fallen. It might rub off."

"I'm not so good, Eden."

"Don't make me laugh! Our parents think you're perfect."

"No really. I . . . have a secret, too."

I don't know why I needed to tell her. Maybe I thought she, of all people, might understand. I unstuck my dry lips from my braces, took a deep breath and began. "I . . . don't believe that God exists."

Eden arched her perfect, dark eyebrows, took a drag of her cigarette, then let out the smoke with a long, low whistle.

"Go on," she said.

I told her how I think it happened. I was doing a school project on Greek myths. I loved the stories, but it suddenly struck me that they weren't just stories to people long ago. They believed they were true. Then I thought, all over the world, every culture has believed something different, and who are we to say we're right? Maybe some girl in the future might read our Bible stories and wonder how on earth we could have believed them.

I told her these thoughts came slowly at first, like fruit rotting, one bruise at a time. Then one Sunday at supper, between first course and dessert, it came in a sudden revelation that I'd lost my faith. As I watched Dad dig into his pie, I just saw some kind of . . . shaman, or witch doctor, or medicine man. Holy to those who believe in God, but silly to those who don't.

I stopped there because Eden was laughing.

"Thinking your parents are misguided comes with being twelve," she said. "Then you get to be my age and you *know* they are!"

I sort of laughed, too, but just on the outside. I hadn't explained myself very well. I hadn't told her that I wished things could be the way they were before, that I hated looking inside myself and finding only questions. Questions I couldn't ask my parents because Mom would have a fit, and Dad—well, Dad's reaction would be even worse. He'd be so sad and disappointed in me.

"I don't know what to say, Mandy. I thought *I* had problems, but you're *really* up a creek. A minister's daughter who doesn't believe in God! Even *I* believe in God. You're living a lie!"

"I know," I whispered.

"Well, come on, little heathen," said Eden, getting to her feet and replacing the tin. "It's time we headed back."

I was afraid to talk as we hiked back home. I felt like a kid again, not knowing if Eden was my friend or enemy. She was like Snow White and the evil queen all rolled up in one person. One minute, she was sweetness and light, and the next she was offering me a poisoned apple.

The minute we walked in the back door, Uncle Mark began sniffing.

"It's wood smoke you smell, Dad, you ol' hound dog," giggled Eden. "We passed some heathens dancing naked round a fire. Oh, don't worry! I didn't look, but Mandy couldn't help herself. She was fascinated by their—uh—reading material. Greek myths, wasn't it, Mand?"

What a perfect name you have, Eden, I thought. An earthly paradise, with a serpent wrapped around its heart.

That fall, Eden ran away from home. It took three trips out west for Aunt Christy and Uncle Mark to find her in Vancouver, and when they did, she said she wasn't coming home. Ever. I heard Mom talking to Aunt Christy on the phone:

"No, thank God, we don't have to worry about Mandy," she said. "We *are* lucky. She's a good, good girl."

When I turned sixteen last year, my first thought was, Eden was this old when she left home. Running away was the last thing I wanted to do. For the first time in my life, I was truly happy. My braces came off. I got contact lenses. I made the cheerleading team and best of all, I had friends. Good friends. Wonderful friends. Friends who kept me so busy I didn't have time to worry about things like not believing in God.

It's hard not to gush when I talk about Kate and Alex and Jewel. I feel like I was searching for my place in the universe and they helped me find it.

They're on the cheerleading team, too. Kate's the captain. She chose me at the tryouts last year and taught me all the moves, even when she had to stay late after practice to help me. She got me a part in the mock royal wedding, too, the day that turned out to be the highlight of my life. It was like stepping into the pages of a fairy tale. There were men in uniforms with swords at their sides, and horse drawn carriages, and dainty little pastries served on silver trays.

Kate was Queen Elizabeth, Alex was Princess Anne, Jewel was Lady Diana, and I got to be her bridesmaid. It was such fun dressing up, like being a kid again, except this time I got to wear a dream of a dress made of real, ivory silk. I don't think even Eden would have called me an ugly duckling that day.

Dad says my friends are great. Mom liked them, too, although she wasn't thrilled about me being a cheerleader. Not when she found out how short the skirts were, and that we had to do cartwheels in them. So I was surprised when she said I could go with the girls for an overnight to Toronto. She got very stiff and quiet when I asked her. Then finally she said, "You're a good girl, Mandy. We trust you." When Mom turned away for a minute, Dad tucked an extra fifty dollars into my pocket and whispered, "Have a nice time, Mandy. You deserve it."

The only rule for our Night to Remember, as we called it, was that we had to do stuff we couldn't (or wouldn't!) do in Lee. The other girls wanted to go out for an elegant, gourmet dinner, and maybe afterward go ballroom dancing, the kind that made their boyfriends gag if they even suggested it. Jewel was an expert at the tango, and she had given us all lessons. What I wanted to do most was go for a swim in the indoor-outdoor pool at our hotel, The Sheraton. I couldn't imagine being able to swim outside in February!

I'd never stayed in a hotel, so I had nothing to compare it to, but it seemed like a palace to me. A lobby of marble and glass. A porter who placed our bags on a cart and guided us up to our room.

I brought one small, overnight bag. The others each brought two huge suitcases. I couldn't believe all the stuff they unpacked. Fancy, lace bras with matching panties. Stockings with rhinestones at the ankles. Earrings that dangled, necklines that dipped, curling irons, blow dryers, makeup kits.

"I look like the poor cousin," I laughed.

"Uh-huh," said Jewel, giggling with the others. "This is for you." What a dress she pulled out! It was even more beautiful than the one I wore for the royal wedding, a real Cinderella dress. It was white chiffon with silver threads woven through it, and a full skirt that flew straight out when I twirled. I felt like I was wearing a cloud. Jewel did my hair, Alex did my makeup and Kate loaned me some earrings that sparkled like real diamonds. I hardly recognized myself when they were done.

I had to wear my own grey shoes because the ones that matched the dress didn't fit me, but Alex pinned a silver flower to the toe of each one to make them look special. I hung my plain, grey dress in the closet, and felt like I was sticking my old self in there, too. A new girl was going out with the girls in the big city. Not Mandy, or Mand. That night, I was Amanda.

We ate dinner in a restaurant filled with dark wood and mirrors and leafy plants that made Kate sneeze. The ceiling with its stained glass dome was as pretty as any church I'd seen. We skipped the main course and ordered a bunch of different appetizers and desserts and sweet, ice-creamy cocktails.

"What if they ask for ID?" I whispered to the others.

"They won't," hissed Alex. "Just look at yourself!"

I peeked in one of the mirrors. Alex was right. I looked at least nineteen.

After supper, we walked up Yonge Street two by two, like kids on a school trip. Kate told me not to stare, that it made me look like a hick. But there was so much to see! In Lee, most people dress from the Sears catalogue. Nothing too wild, nothing that might draw attention. But here! There were punks and preps, fur coats and rags, men holding hands with men, and women holding hands with women.

I wondered if these people had once been trapped in small towns like mine, and run away to where they could be themselves. I thought about Eden.

Until I saw The Man. We all saw him. I could almost hear our four hearts go *thump* at the same time. He looked as if he had stepped off the cover of a paperback romance that was tucked under someone's arm. He was about six-foot-five, with shoulders as broad as a river and yellow hair that flowed down his back. He wore jeans and a leather jacket, but even with all those clothes on, you could see his muscles pushing at the seams. Not just a man, I thought, a prince of men! A god. Adonis.

"He looks like a body builder," whispered Alex.

"Maybe he's going to a gym," said Kate. "Look at his gym bag."

"Keep walking," Jewel giggled. "He's getting away!"

We followed him for three blocks, staying far enough back so we could whisper.

"Oh man, look at the way he walks," Alex moaned.

"Shhh, you guys!" said Kate. "You're shocking Mandy."

"No, you're not," I said.

"We shouldn't be doing this," said Jewel. "We're all attached."

"You're right," said Alex. "Except for Mandy."

They decided to "get" him for me, whatever that meant.

"No!" I hissed. I had trouble telling when people were serious or joking.

They laughed and speeded up, closing the gap between us and Adonis. Suddenly he disappeared through a door. The front door of a strip club. The sidewalk in front was littered with cigarette butts and flattened wads of gum. Just to stand outside such a place filled me with a thrilling sense of wickedness.

Posted on the wall were pictures of the dancers. It looked like a costume party. There was a cowgirl, a peacock, a cheerleader. We giggled at that one. Her skirt wasn't much shorter than ours.

"Ooo . . . look!" whispered Jewel. "There are guys, too."

Further down the wall were posters of male dancers.

"Maybe that's what was in his gym bag!" whispered Alex. "A costume!" We shuffled closer to look for Adonis, but his picture wasn't there.

"I'm having a wicked idea," said Kate.

"Me too," said Jewel.

"Oh my God," said Alex, giggling. "Should we?"

"Mandy, do you want to?" asked Kate. "We won't if you don't want to."

They looked at me. If I said no, I knew they wouldn't mind. But I didn't want to say no. Two ladies pushed past us and opened the double doors. Inside, I saw lights blinking in the darkness, and smoke, and the tattooed bicep of a bouncer. I could hear Mom's voice saying: *Wide is the gate, and broad is the way, that leadeth to destruction.* Then I took a deep breath and said: "C'mon. Let's go in."

It took a moment for my eyes to adjust to the darkness. I grabbed the back of Kate's coat and followed her down the stairs. Music was blaring so loud we had to shout just to hear each other. Strobe lights flashed, lighting up a smoky sea of arms that waved back and forth in time to the music. I saw dim shapes along the walls that looked like portholes and anchors. I guess we were supposed to be below the decks of a ship, but I had a sinking feeling that we'd descended into hell.

We ordered a round of drinks, beer this time. Our waiter wore skintight pants and a pirate shirt open to the waist. He set the glass of beer in front of me and winked. I panicked. Was he a dancer? Would I be seeing him naked? Was this really beer, or was it poison, or drugged to turn me into one of the whooping, hollering women around us? Why were my shoes stuck to the floor? Would I catch a disease and have to tell my parents where I was?

Eden was right that day by the stream. I was scared of everything. Where was my brave, wicked self that had marched through the front doors of this place?

"Relax," whispered Jewel. Kate and Alex reached across the table to pat my hands. The first dancer swivelled onto the dance floor.

He wasn't Adonis or Prince Charming or anyone one else from my daydreams. He looked almost as old as my Dad, and his dancing was too fast, too frantic. It was embarrassing, not sexy.

But Alex, Kate and Jewel were laughing and clapping, so I clapped along with them. Beads of sweat spiralled off the dancer, turning red in the lights. At the end of the song, he gyrated off the dance floor and swivelled between the tables, heading straight for us. Thank God he was still wearing a G-string. Alex and Jewel squealed and covered their eyes. I pretended I was fishing something out of my drink. But Kate watched, thanked him politely, and gave him a five dollar bill when he was done. Kate could keep her head in a twister.

I needed fresh air. Alex came with me to the bathroom. We groped our way through the sea of hooting women, and collapsed on the chairs in the ladies' room.

"Phew!" said Alex. "What do you think so far?"

"Very . . . educational!" I said. We both cracked up.

An exotic creature stepped out of a stall, and set her wine glass down on the counter. She wore five-inch stiletto heels, a feathered mask, and a costume that shimmered with green and gold scales. I must have been staring because she turned toward me. There was something familiar about her glittering smile, her green eyes that sparkled like jewels behind the mask.

"If it isn't Mandy Solesby!" she laughed. "Do your parents know you're here?"

I thought I'd never see Eden again. I'd imagined her many ways, usually looking lost and pathetic in the corner of some rat-infested room. Not like this. She looked . . . larger than life.

"It must be the Judgement Day to see you in this place," she sneered. "Come, let's get a look at you." She pulled me to my feet and turned me toward the mirror. Her reflection towered above mine. She must have been six feet tall in those heels.

"Aren't we a pair!" she laughed. "The great whore bedecked with precious stones, her golden cup filled with the filthiness of fornication. And the bride of the Lamb, clothed in white raiment, for she is a virgin . . . I would assume."

I recognized her words from the Book of Revelation. I'd always loved that book of the Bible, with its fabulous images of the end of this world and the beginning of the next. Paradise, but this time it was a city, not a garden.

I loved what Jesus said to John: *I am Alpha and Omega, the beginning and the ending, which is, and which was, and which is to come.* Eden had been there in the beginning, for me. Was this night to be my end?

"I have to run," said Eden. "I'm on upstairs in a minute. Come see the show if you like."

"I've . . . uh . . . got some friends down here."

"I'm sure you do! Well, I'll see you around. If not in this life,

then the next. You'll be there with the rest of the liars and unbe-
lievers, lined up to jump in the lake of fire and brimstone, right?
Well, see ya there."

I couldn't say a word as she left, but I felt Alex's hand on my
arm.

"*Who* was that?" she whispered.

"My cousin, Eden. And please, Alex, *please* don't tell the others you saw her, okay?"

"Why not? She was a riot!"

"I don't want anyone to know." If any of this got back to my
parents, or Eden's, I was afraid it would kill them.

Alex didn't tell, although I was afraid it might slip out later, in
the hotel room. We were playing Truth or Dare and had to tell
the others what we were most ashamed of. It was a special
moment, sitting cross-legged on the bed with my friends, by the
light of one small lamp. One by one, they told things that I knew
were hard for them to say. Things that afterward, I wished I did-
n't know. Some secrets aren't meant to be told.

When my turn came, I couldn't tell them that I didn't believe
in God, and that my whole existence as Reverend Solesby's perfect
daughter was a lie. Part of me wanted to, but part of me remembered confiding in Eden that day, and how she turned on me.
Because I wouldn't tell, they dared me to swim naked in the hotel
pool while they stood guard. I didn't mind. It let me off the hook,
and let me do something I knew they'd respect if I pulled it off.

By some miracle, the hotel staff had left the door to the
swimming pool unlocked. The room reeked of chlorine. It was
dark, but small lights shone underwater, and moonlight shone in
from outside. I dropped my robe to the floor and dove in. For the
first time in my life, I was skinny dipping. Eden had done it at
Dorey Lake, but I never would in case my father or uncle saw me.
It felt wonderful, like having a bath, only better.

The girls cheered quietly from the deck. Suddenly I needed to be alone. I swam under the barrier, and floated on my back out-doors. There wasn't a star in sight, just an orange haze that arched like a dome above the city. I opened and closed my arms and legs. My breath joined the steam rising off the water. Thick, soft snowflakes began to fall and melt on my cheeks, like tears.

Two months later, in April, my mother died of a heart attack. As far as I know, she never knew that I went to a strip club, or drank too much alcohol, or went skinny dipping in a public swimming pool. As far as I know, she died still thinking I was a perfect daughter.

People say she was so heavy, her heart just gave out, but I don't buy that. She was only thirty-nine! She should have lived to be seventy, or eighty, or ninety! She should have lived to see my wedding, and the birth of my child in a room filled with flowers and baskets of fruit.

It's May now, but it still doesn't seem real. I expect her to walk through the door, or call on the phone, making excuses for why she's been away so long. I feel like she's been off at a conference or a holiday, up in Dorey Lake maybe, getting ready for the reunion, gossiping in Aunt Christy's kitchen over cups of herbal tea.

Even the funeral didn't make it seem real. Dad gave a beautiful eulogy and got through most of it without breaking down. He said spring was a time for new beginnings. He said we're like cater-pillars during our time on earth, and death is our metamorphosis, when we're freed to become something greater. I wish I believed like Dad believes. I wish I believed Mom's spirit is as free as a but-terfly. I really do. But when I close my eyes and think of her, I don't see the flutter of wings against a blue sky. I see a closed cof-fin lid and a hole in the ground, six feet deep. I see darkness and nothingness. I don't see a new beginning. I see only an ending.

"Mandy? Mandy, honey?"

"Yes, Dad?"

"You've been staring at that page for nearly twenty minutes."

"Have I?" I see that I've written just one sentence: *In the beginning, there was Eden.*

"Are you all right?" he asks.

"I guess so . . . Oh . . . Dad."

Finally, the words spill out of me and fill up the space between us. As the miles roll past, I tell Dad about Eden, in the beginning, when I worshipped her, and in the middle, when I told her I lost my faith, and at the end, when I saw her that night in Toronto.

I stare straight ahead as I talk, certain I'll shock him into swerving off the road, but nothing I say seems to faze him. Now and then, he reaches over to pat my clammy hand.

"Fire and brimstone, eh?" he chuckles. "That Eden. Mandy . . . I wish you'd talked to me sooner. To think it's been eating you up all this time, and I never even realized. It's like your mother used to say—the doctor's child never gets the pill."

I can't talk. If I do, I'll cry.

"Mandy, my love. Do you think I've never struggled with my faith? Surely you've heard Uncle Mark say what a wild kid I was?"

"Yes . . . but I never knew you questioned your faith."

"Oh, I did! Questioned it long and hard, and for a few years I really put God to the test, did some pretty awful things—"

"Like going to a strip club?"

"Yes," he laughs, "among other things. I'll tell you sometime if you want to know. But the point is, Mandy, that God didn't give up on me. Just as He won't give up on you or even Eden. It's a father's unconditional love for his child, a bond beyond words. . . ."

Now I really am crying, but not because I'm sad.

"Faith is like that, beyond words," Dad continues. "It's hard to talk about, even harder to convince someone. It's just . . . there.

You feel it. You know it. Sometimes I think of faith as a tree that gets lost in the forest, and one day you stumble upon it and give it a bit of water and care, and then it grows like crazy. Maybe your tree's just lost for now, Mandy."

"You think I'll find it, Dad?"

"I think so . . . I know so," he winks at me and laughs. "It has strong roots."

Suddenly I realize that we've turned off the main road. "Are we lost?"

"No," he says. "I just thought we'd mosey this trip. No need to rush. I'm enjoying being with my girl. . . . You hungry? This looks like a nice picnic spot."

"It's perfect."

Dad pulls over beside a large field that has a wonderfully ancient-looking tree root fence. We pick our way through it, and walk through the long grass toward the stream at the far end. My scalp tingles in the heat, and the same hypnotic feeling I used to get when Eden brushed out my hair comes over me. I want to cry out loud, *I told him! I told him, and he still loves me!*

Weeping willows bend over the stream, trailing branches in the water like long, lazy fingertips. When I look up, the higher branches arch above me like a cathedral. I can almost feel God in this place.

"Dad? This field reminds me of the twenty-third psalm."

He smiles and nods. It's the psalm he read at Mom's funeral.

*The Lord is my shepherd; I shall not want. He maketh me to lie down in green pastures: he leadeth me beside the still waters. He restoreth my soul. . . .* We recite it together, quietly, while we lay out our picnic.

We dangle our feet in the stream while we eat. Dad congratulates me on the excellent peanut butter sandwiches. I compliment him on the delicious apples and cheese. Then he lays back on the moss and pushes his hat over his face. Dad likes a rest after eating.

But I jump up and wade into the stream. I want to know what's beyond the curtain of willow branches.

"Dad?"

"Hmm?"

"I'm just going upstream a ways."

"Take your time, honey," Dad mumbles sleepily. "I'm not going anywhere."

## the puzzle

# (Naylor)

I finish the map quiz early and slap it answer-side down on the left-hand corner of my desk, the way Miss Twitchit likes. She smiles at me from her desk, then looks back down at the thick geology book that's propped up in front of her. From the way she's sucking so hard on her candy and looking so pink in the cheeks, I wonder if she's got a steamy romance novel tucked between the covers.

Kids in the class pull that trick on her all the time, especially the Neanderthals in the back row—except what they're reading is definitely x-rated. I was unlucky enough to surprise them one day when they were trading porn magazines behind the portables, and they roughed me up pretty bad. Now they pick on me every chance they get: "Hey, *Dumbo,* can you stop flappin' your *ears?* The wind is messin' up my hair," or "Hey *Whitehead!* Been eatin' too much pizza . . . *face?*"

Someday I'll get my pilot's license and fly far away from this redneck town. That's my dream—to have clear skin and ears that lie flat against my head. To look so cool in my aviator jacket and parachute that the girls beg me, "Nayl, please take us with you. . . ."

A chair scrapes back, and Jewel Jackman squeezes past, heading up to Miss Twitchit's desk to ask a question. I breathe in as she walks past. I love the way Jewel smells of baby powder, not perfume. Today she's wearing a pink T-shirt and white jeans, and her underwear must be pink, too because it's blushing right through the seat of her pants, as if they see me staring. Get a life, Nayl. Jewel's underwear don't know you exist. But at least the rest of her does. She actually spoke to me today after Mr. Reid's English class. Reid was talking about Zen stuff again and Jewel must have seen me looking miserable because she came up to me in the hall and said, "Are you having trouble with the haiku poem, too?" I was so surprised, and she smelled so good, it took me a second to find something to say.

"Yeah," is what I came up with.

This haiku assignment is driving me crazy. It should be so easy—only three lines long, five syllables in the first line, seven in the second, five in the third. Seventeen syllables, that's it. It doesn't even have to rhyme. Easy, right? Wrong.

Reid says a true Zen haiku should "enlighten" him. "Blow him away" was how he put it. He says it should feel like a bomb going off in his head, or at least like someone's clicked on a light. If we can teach him something, or make him see something in a different way, we pass. If we don't, we fail. The haiku's worth a third of our final grade and I'm not doing very well in that class. Reid doesn't believe in what he calls the "memorization and regurgitation" method of teaching. Unfortunately, that's just the kind of class I like. Give me some notes and a textbook to study and I'll give you an "A." Ask me to write a Zen haiku, and I'm lost.

"I might try writing a koan," I said to Jewel. "I'm better at puzzles than poetry." Reid said if we're feeling very Zen, we can hand in a koan instead of a haiku. The way he explains it, a koan is a riddle that forces you to throw out logic and think with your intuition. It should be so hard to understand that you feel like you're banging your head against a wall, but when you finally "get it" you're on your way to enlightenment. Then you can rest, I guess, (and bandage your head).

Jewel seemed genuinely impressed. "Wow! I think the koan would be even harder to write. You need a special kind of mind to do that."

Mom said something similar when I came home with my last two jigsaw puzzles—an all-red blob of paint and a 3 x 3" puzzle with pieces so small I need Mom's eyebrow tweezers to put it together. "You need a certain kind of mind to do those," she said, shaking her head. I don't think it was a compliment. But when Jewel said what she did, it sounded as if she could see past my Dumbo ears and bad skin to the brain inside my head, and unless I'm mistaken, Jewel thinks my brain is okay.

On her way back to her desk, Jewel smiles at me. Now I'm more determined than ever to write a good haiku or koan for Reid. I'll make a bomb go off in his head, in honor of beautiful Jewel.

"Naylor? . . . Naylor Whitehead? Could you open a window, please?"

Miss Twitchit sure knows how to snap a guy out of his daydream. It *is* hot in here, but to open the window, I'll have to show the huge sweat stains under my arms that I've been hiding so carefully all period. I shove up the window and wait for the insults from the back row: *Nice pits, Whitehead.* I do hear whispers, but when I turn around I realize it's not me people are staring at.

There's a new guy standing in the doorway. People are gawking at the poor guy as if he just stepped off a spaceship. He's got long black hair tied into a ponytail, and skin the color of polished maple. He's wearing a faded red leather shirt and army fatigues—a lot of clothes for such a hot day although I notice he's not sweating. I guess the girls think he's good-looking. The whole front row sits up straighter and starts flicking their hair over their shoulders.

"Miss Twitchit?" he says with a perfect English accent.

Miss Twitchit nearly spills her tea. Twitchit warns everyone that she suffers from a disease called Anglophilia, and if they utter one word of criticism about Britain, they risk failing geography class. She's not really joking either. There's a Union Jack hanging on one wall of her classroom, a map of the British Isles on another wall, and over the blackboard is a portrait of Queen Elizabeth, looking as cool as only a queen can be when this sauna of a classroom reaches ninety degrees. No matter how hot it gets, Miss Twitchit sips tea all period long from one of two mugs—her Chuck-and-Di mug from the real royal wedding (when she travelled to London and camped outside St. Paul's Cathedral to catch a glimpse of them,) or the Jewel-and-Derek mug from the mock royal wedding Miss Twitchit organized last year.

It's the real mug she almost spills when she hears the new guy's accent.

"Why . . . yes?"

"I'm Juan Delacosa." He hands her a note on pink office paper, which she reads while dabbing her forehead with her hanky.

"Right. Welcome to the class, Juan. You may sit beside Naylor. He'll fill you in. We've been discussing cartography. Now, class, settle down and pass your test papers forward, please."

By now, I'm sure most people have whispered the answers to each other. Miss Twitchit gathers the tests into a tidy pile, tucks them into a folder and hands back our maps from last week. I get an A. Miss Twitchit loves my maps. I never mix up my longitude with my latitude and I never color outside the lines.

The new guy, Juan, smiles at me when he sits down, glances at my map, and pulls out an old-fashioned pencil box with a sliding lid. He draws for the rest of the period, and he seems so into it, I doubt he hears a word Miss Twitchit says. It's a map he's drawing, but not like any I've seen before. It's an island with a mountain range down one side. His mountains aren't upside down V's like mine. They're shaded and snow-capped and seem to rise right off the page. Pouring off the mountains are rivers— angry white water crashing down so hard I can almost feel the spray. In the waves offshore two vicious-looking sea serpents writhe and battle to the death. The only calm place on the whole map is a small inland lake with a tiny red sailboat bobbing on it. All this, he creates on an 8½ x 11" piece of paper. Just watching him draw it wears me out. I'm drenched with sweat by the time the bell rings.

"I guess you don't need longitude and latitude in a world like that, eh?" I say.

"No," he laughs quietly. "I've never been good at straight lines."

Then he's surrounded by girls asking him where's he's from and what classes he's in and I figure that's the end of all conversations with social leper Naylor Whitehead. But it turns out he's in all my classes but English, and in every one he sits down in the empty seat beside me. I can see the girls sizing me up as if they missed seeing something before. Maybe they figure if the cool new guy thinks I'm okay, there's more to me than they thought. It's hard to tell if Juan likes all the attention he's getting, or if he even notices. He sure never looks at the girls the way he looks at his maps.

He draws maps in every class. He's got it down to a fine art— not just the way he draws but the way he hides what he's doing, sliding down in his seat, holding his binder upright, concentrating so hard the teachers must not want to disturb him. He draws all kinds of places, none of them real. Rain forests with flying monkeys, deserts littered with dragon skeletons and ghostly white snake skins, even an underwater treasure map. But on every map, whether there's water or not, he puts in the little red sailboat. When I ask him about it, he just shrugs. It's a trademark, I figure, like the happy faces some girls put in their O's.

He only gets into trouble once, in math class, when he's concentrating particularly hard on a map and keeps missing what the teacher's saying to him. He gets sent down to the office. Later he tells me that they accused him of being stoned.

"They couldn't be more wrong," he said. "I'd never touch pot. Or anything else."

One day Miss Twitchit asks us both to stay after class. It's another sweltering day. She gets her hanky out to sop up her "glow," which is what she calls sweat. She says that exams are coming up and she's worried that Juan's not absorbing everything.

"A bit of a daydreamer, aren't you?" she says. So she did know what was going on behind his binder. "Perhaps Naylor could help you prepare for exams."

He nods, "Okay."

"Fine . . . oh—and Juan? I looked up something the other day. Your name rang a bell—"

For the first time, I see Juan break a sweat. Just like that, beads of sweat pop out on his upper lip.

"I'm not sure if you're aware of this, but you share the name of an early cartographer, Juan de la Cosa. He sailed on the Santa Maria with Christopher Columbus."

"That's so cool!" I say. "Maybe you're related."

"I wouldn't know," says Juan. He looks relieved for some reason.

"Are you of Spanish descent?" asks Miss Twitchit.

Juan smiles. "Sort of. One quarter Spanish, one quarter English, one quarter Native American, and . . . one quarter's a mystery."

Miss Twitchit glows even more, not just with sweat but with something else, too—pride maybe? As if she was thinking: *I knew it! A geographic wonder in my very own classroom!*

Juan and I decide to study at my house because it's close to the school and there's usually something not too mouldy to munch on in the fridge. The kitchen table's covered with Mom's craft paints, so we grab some cookies and head down the hall to my room, the only clean room in the house. I have to keep it tidy so I don't lose any puzzle pieces. Juan stops dead in the doorway and I realize how lame this must look—three puzzles partly done on my worktable, and dozens more stacked in boxes on my shelves. I know teenage guys shouldn't be sitting at home doing jigsaw puzzles. They should be out *doing*. But I guess I'm kind of addicted.

Juan goes right to the big puzzle that's mounted on the wall and runs his fingers around the outside edge. It's shaped like a space shuttle, and it looks like one, too, but up close you can see other pictures hidden inside the big one—pictures of the great pioneer flyers like the Wright brothers with their first plane, and Charles Lindbergh with the Spirit of St. Louis that he flew across the Atlantic Ocean, and Amelia Earhart with her Lockheed Electra that she used for her round-the-world flight. I love that puzzle. It gives me hope.

"Fantastic," Juan whispers.

So I show him the others I'm working on—the blob of red paint, and the tiny 3 x 3" one. He likes the picture on that one, an Escher painting of people at the top of a tower going up and down a square set of stairs. It's an optical illusion because they never get anywhere. The up becomes down, the down becomes up, and the people just keep going round and round. But the puzzle he pores over longest is the one I just started—a wizard's workshop where the walls and shelves and tables are covered with clocks set at different times, and compasses pointing in different directions.

I glance at my own watch and notice that half an hour has ticked by and we haven't begun to study yet. "Juan? Maybe we should get started. . . ."

"Would your mum mind if we used some of those paints?"

he asks, staring at the blank wall beside my bed.

"What, for studying geography?"

He grins. "Sort of."

It takes us less than two hours to completely transform my bedroom wall. Juan does most of the painting, I just fill in blocks of color where he tells me to. When we're done, it's the coolest thing I've ever seen. It's a painting of a clock, but it's a map, too. The perimeter of the clock is a shoreline, and instead of numbers on the face, there are islands. Islands within an island, and each one is different. One is a pair of cupped hands, another is a pair of lips puckered into a volcano shape. One island is covered with jagged rocks, another has smooth rolling hills. One is shaped like a key, another like an apple. He leaves one of the islands blank except for a grey mist swirling around it. But the part I like best is what he paints at the ends of the clock's hands—an airplane at the end of one, and a red sailboat at the end of the other. With a tiny brush he paints a name on the sailboat: *Freedom.*

At first I have to keep reminding myself that normal people do spontaneous things and don't always study when they're supposed to. Besides, we're talking about geography as we paint . . . sort of. Juan tells me about England, where he lived with his mother in a cottage with flowers growing inside and out.

"And suns! Mum made clay pots that looked like suns—yellow summer suns and winter suns and red sunset suns. . . ."

I'm not surprised to hear that Juan's mother was an artist, but I am surprised to hear she was Buddhist. Juan says that's the main reason his father took off while Juan was a baby—because of his "philosophical differences" with his mother.

"We're different all right," says Juan, smacking the paintbrush hard against the wall. "I hated it when I had to come live with him after Mum died. He was a stranger to me. Still is."

"Same with me and my dad. The only thing we have in common is our name. Naylor Whitehead. Lucky me, eh? I see him twice a year—at Christmas and my birthday."

"That's two more times a year than I'd like to see my father. . . . Let's talk about something else, okay?"

"Sure. . . ." I dig around in my brain for a safe topic, like school. Haiku assignments. "Juan? Since your mom was a Buddhist, did she teach you about Zen haikus and koans and stuff?"

From his blank look, I can tell he doesn't have a clue what I'm talking about, so I tell him about Mr. Reid's assignment. But Juan can't tell me much. He says he remembers his mother meditating a lot and telling him stories about people who were so good at meditation that they could leave their bodies and fly through walls as if they were mist.

"Yeah, Reid talked about that," I say. "If you're really enlightened you can do that stuff. Maybe my koan will send Reid flying into orbit, eh? Do you think your mom really believed people can do that?"

"I don't know . . . but think about all the kids in books who find different worlds just by opening a door or stepping into a painting, and all the stories about alien abductions by little grey men, and near-death experiences where you see a tunnel of light. Maybe so many stories are the same because there's something true about them."

"So you think you can step into a painting and show up in another place?"

"Well . . . no. But it would be nice." Then he changes the subject. He taps the island that looks like a pair of lips. "So tell me about Jewel," he says. "Have you liked her long?"

"Is it obvious?"

"Sort of."

"Great. Well, I guess I've liked her for . . . two years or so." More like since kindergarten, but I don't tell him that.

"She has a boyfriend, you know."

"Jake. Yeah, I know. They act like they're married already. I wouldn't stand a chance anyway, but . . . you can't blame a guy for wishing, can you?"

"No. . . . Why is her face on Miss Twitchit's mug?"

I laugh. "That, my friend, was the infamous mock royal wedding of 1982. You're probably the only person in the township who hasn't heard of it." Juan looks confused. "It started out as a show the high school was going to put on instead of the usual play," I explain, "but Miss Twitchit took over organizing it—she's nuts about royal stuff—and a couple of big businesses kicked in some money, so it ended up being pretty splashy. I was in it, you know. You're looking at the one and only Accidental Prince."
Juan still looks confused.

"I'd been at every rehearsal, helping with the lights, so I guess I knew most of the parts. On the day of the show, the guy who was supposed to play Prince Edward broke his foot. Miss Twitchit hauled me backstage, said I was the perfect size for the suit and suddenly I was walking down the aisle. She still sometimes calls me the 'Accidental Prince.' It was fun, actually. Jewel was Diana. I got to spend a whole day hanging around her."

Juan opens the lid on the yellow paint and with a few brush strokes puts a crown around the island with the volcano lips. We both laugh. That's when Mom comes in.

I hadn't heard her come through the front door, but suddenly she's standing in my doorway staring at the paint all over my hands and the mural on the wall. She looks about to blow. Mom's not much of a housekeeper, but she doesn't like changes to the house, and wall murals done with her own craft paints qualify as change. Major change.

Then she registers that there's someone else in my room and her whole face goes mushy, as if she's just found her little boy making friends in the finger-painting corner at preschool. Before she can run for her camera to capture the moment on film, I introduce them.

Mom falls under Juan's spell as soon as she hears his accent, just like Miss Twitchit did. What is it with women and accents? I make a mental note that Nayl in my dream should have an accent, French maybe. Mom invites Juan to stay for dinner, but he says he has to get home. His dad doesn't like to eat alone. I can see Mom making mental calculations. If Juan's father is as charming as his son, maybe we should *all* get together for dinner.

"So where exactly is 'home'?" asks Mom. She's a real estate agent and knows just about every house in town.

"Banton Lane," says Juan.

"Oh? There are some nice new bungalows there. Which one is yours?"

"It's not one of the new houses. It's an old farmhouse right at the end."

"Oh! I rented that one. . . . That was your *father?*"

I glare at Mom for sounding so rude, but after Juan leaves, she warns me to be careful. "His father really gave me the creeps. How well do you really know this boy?"

I don't know him well at all, I realize. We sit together in class. We've talked about maps and puzzles and Jewel and Zen Buddhism and a bit about our parents, but even after all that, Juan is still a mystery. He doesn't show up at school the next day, or the next, and there's no answer when I call his home number. I decide to walk over to Banton Lane to see if he's all right.

Banton Lane is one of the new streets at the edge of town. There are three brick bungalow designs built along it. The model homes have signs with names on them: "The Katie," "The Suzy," "The Kelly." Some of them have grass and small trees planted. Others just have lawns of mud, but there are lots of kids around drawing pictures and hopscotch squares on the sidewalk with big pieces of chalk. A police officer is leaning against a stop sign talking to a couple of parents. Her name's Janet. She's come to our school for Safety Week. I wonder what she'd say about going to creepy old farmhouses where no one answers the phone.

As the house numbers decrease, so do the number of people outside. The last two blocks are older models of bungalows with dark frowning porches and no one outside except the odd yawning cat. Juan's house is at the end, behind a row of ratty spruce trees. It's a crazy-looking house, the kind you'd imagine an inventor would live in, with a tangle of antennas on the roof and boxlike additions on the sides and upper story. I count three doors on the second floor that open onto thin air.

A line of rusty old cars slouches along one side of the house. I feel their empty eye sockets glaring at me as I walk up to the sagging front porch. There's duct tape covering the doorbell, so I knock. No answer. I knock again, louder. I try peeking through the narrow window beside the door, but it's covered with newspaper on the inside. Just like Mom said, it's creepy. Ninety percent of my body wants to turn around and run, but by now I'm more than just curious about Juan. I'm worried.

I walk along the side of the house. From what I can see, every window is covered with paper. I wonder if Juan's dad has an aversion to light. More of the ratty spruce trees are growing beside and behind the house. I smell something sweet, not spruce or pine, but a natural kind of smell. It's very quiet back here. No children playing, no skateboard wheels scraping along the sidewalk . . . just the odd cricket chirping, the faint whir of a distant motor . . . and a muffled angry shout.

Logic makes me want to run back to the street. Intuition makes me run to the back of the house. It's a graveyard of junk back there. Old cars and car parts, milk cans, tires, old doors and broken windows, and what looks like the skeleton of a kite. I hear the shout again, louder, coming from the basement. It's not Juan's voice.

There are two basement windows, both covered with newspaper, but one has a corner where the paper inside has peeled back. I kneel down to look. It's not at all what I expected to see in the basement of an old house like this. It's filled with light and looks like a greenhouse with rows of plants. Some are seedlings in small white pots. Some are mature plants, and it's on those that I see the shape of the leaves. I've seen pictures of marijuana leaves on T-shirts at school, and I'm pretty sure that's what I'm seeing in the basement. It must be something illegal anyway. Why else would the windows be blocked up?

Then I see Juan standing still as a statue against the stone wall of the basement. He's wearing the same clothes he had on the day I met him—the red leather shirt and army fatigues, except now his feet are bare and his hair is hanging loose around his face. A big hulking guy—who I assume is his father—is waving his arms and yelling at him. I wonder what Juan did to make him so mad because right now he's doing nothing. Maybe Juan being so still and calm is exactly what's driving his dad so wild. His dad pounds the wall beside Juan's face. Juan doesn't flinch. He even smiles a little. I wonder if maybe he's stoned, but I doubt it. He said he never touches the stuff. He's probably just off somewhere in his mind, drawing a map, meditating. If I had to live with the Incredible Hulk, I'd probably check out mentally, too.

But his dad's not happy just hitting the wall. He grabs Juan by the shirt collar and shakes him and roars like a wild animal, but Juan's face doesn't change. He looks quiet and calm. With another roar, his dad picks him up like a sack of laundry and tosses him right toward me. For a split second, it seems that Juan's flying through the air in slow motion. I know he sees me at the window. It's as if a light goes on in his face. He's glad I'm here. But how can I help him? There's no latch or handle outside the window. I'll have to smash it—

Juan hits the wall right below me. I hear the thud. I feel the window shudder against my hands. But I don't hear Juan scream. What if he hit his head? His father strides over and yanks Juan to his feet. I see blood on Juan's face and head, but he's still conscious. He even looks at me and smiles a little. His look says, *Don't worry, man.* How can I not worry when his hulking father seems hell-bent on killing him?

I can't hear what his father is yelling. The seal on the window must be tight, and the glass is thick. I look around for something to break it. In the junk pile maybe. . . . His father roars again. I look back. His father has two fists full of Juan's shirt again. He lifts him in the air and throws him once more, against the stone wall where just a few minutes ago Juan was leaning quiet and still as a statue. I wince. God, that's going to hurt. Hurt like I've never felt before. I've only been beat up once, and wound up crying like a baby. I can't imagine my own father throwing me against a stone wall.

Juan's back slams into the wall. His arms and legs are spread out like the X on a treasure map. He's smiling. It must hurt like hell, but he's actually smiling.

And then he's gone.

I don't know what happened. One second he was splayed against the wall, and the next second he should have crumpled to the floor. But he didn't. He's just . . . gone.

I stare at the wall. His dad stares, too. His fists open and close, grasping air. He sags and seems to shrink before my eyes. He runs to the wall and feels along it. Maybe he's looking for an opening, a door, a passageway, somewhere Juan could have slipped through. He's making awful animal sounds again, not roars but moans. Then suddenly he spins around and sees me. His eyes are wild, murderous. Does he think what happened was my fault, that I'm some kind of magician who made Juan disappear? In two strides he's at the window, tearing at the paper.

I run. I run past the junk, past the empty eye sockets of the rust heaps, past the ratty spruce trees. I yell, "SOMEONE CALL THE COPS!" All the way up Banton Lane, I run and yell, past the houses with the invisible neighbors, till I reach the brick bungalows and see Janet climbing into her police cruiser.

I scream her name. She sticks her head out. The kids stop playing and gape. Janet comes running to meet me. I'm panting and must sound incoherent, but I manage to tell her the address and that Juan's father is beating him, bad. I don't tell her that Juan seemed to disappear because that just doesn't make sense. He must be in the basement somewhere. I tell her she better get there fast. And, boy, does she get there fast.

She springs to action as if she's been waiting her whole life for this chance. She yells into her car radio and lays rubber as she squeals off down the street. I stand there for a second not sure what to do. Wouldn't she want me there? Don't I have to give some sort of report? I don't know, but I do want to know if Juan's all right. I take off down the street again with a bunch of kids in tow, all wanting to know what's going on. I don't know what to tell them—my friend's father was beating him to a pulp and then threw him right through a solid stone wall? I end up saying nothing.

We watch from the line of spruce trees as Janet pounds on the front door again and again until Juan's father finally opens up. He doesn't look so huge standing on the porch. He looks as if he's in shock, his face as pale as flour, his eyes hollow.

"Where is your son, sir?" Janet asks.

"He's . . . gone."

Gone? Does he mean dead?

"What do you mean 'gone,' sir?" asks Janet.

I hear the siren of another police car roaring down the street. An ambulance is right behind it. Juan's father looks at them and shakes his head. He starts to cry.

"I don't know. . . . He's just . . . gone. I don't know where he went."

"You mean he ran away?"

He cries hard then. I can't believe it. This brute who not long ago was beating up his son, who is half his size, is sobbing with his face in his hands. Either he's a good actor, or he really is shaken up by what he saw—what *we* saw. But what did I see? I don't know. I don't understand.

The next day at school people treat me like some kind of hero. A crowd gathers around me at lunchtime. I have to tell the story over and over again. Teachers ask; students ask. Jewel asks. I tell them everything, except I skim over the part when Juan seemed to disappear. They think I'm weird enough without giving them more fuel for ridicule.

I do tell Janet, the cop, what I saw, even the part about Juan disappearing. They're tearing the house apart looking for him, but Janet seems to think he's just run away and they'll pick him up in the city or something. She can't tell me exactly how he could have gotten through a solid stone wall.

I sort of float through the next few weeks. I get through exams, not very well. I hand in a pathetically ordinary haiku about apple blossoms and springtime. It's bound to earn me a failing grade. Jewel's haiku is amazing. It's about mothers and babies. She reads it to the class and then announces that the rumors are true—she's pregnant and getting married to Jake. Talk about a bomb going off in my head.

I spend most of my time doing puzzles. I finish the blob of red paint and the tiny Escher puzzle and the wizard's workshop. I don't feel any smarter when I'm done. Next time I get to the city, I'm going to buy one of the new three-tier puzzles that force you to think in dimensions. Maybe what happened to Juan is like a koan, a riddle. You can't figure it out by thinking about it logically. But I don't know how to think any other way. I decide to go back to Juan's house to see if the answer comes to me in a Zen moment of enlightenment.

Of course it doesn't. When I get there, the house just sits and stares at me. The rusty cars don't look scary anymore. They just look like junk. There's police tape up, warning people not to cross the line, but there doesn't seem to be anyone here.

Something looks different about the newspapers covering the glass panel beside the door. I duck under the tape to check it out. It's not English or even our alphabet, but some sort of foreign script I don't recognize. Was Juan's dad Arabic or something? I don't think so. And this newspaper looks brand new, not yellowed like the others. Then I see the photograph. I don't know how I could have missed it. It's Juan. It has to be Juan. He's wearing the same red leather shirt and army fatigues, except now the sleeves and pant legs are cut off. His hair is loose and whipping around his smiling face. He's standing on a beach somewhere, and behind him is a sailboat. I have to squint to read the name: *Freedom.*

He did it. Juan got away. I don't know how, but he did it, just like those Buddhists his mom used to talk about who could fly through walls, and the kids in books who can step through paintings and into other times and places and worlds.

For a second I feel jealous, like the crippled kid left behind when the Pied Piper piped away the other kids. I look again at the photo of Juan. Already it's starting to look yellowed, and the name on the boat is impossible to read. Maybe it's not Juan at all but just my wishful thinking. I put my hand against it. All I feel is cool smooth glass.

When I get home I find a lumpy water-stained package stuffed in the door. I never get mail, but it's addressed to me. The stamps have flying monkeys on them and the name of some country I've never heard of. *Oacsalde.* Inside there's no note, just pieces of a jigsaw puzzle. They're beautiful, hand painted. There's no question the puzzle's from Juan.

I take it to my room and spread out the pieces. It doesn't take long to put it together. The picture's of an island with white sand beaches and softly bending palm trees. A small crowd of cheering people are gathered on the beach, waving wildly at a small airplane that's coming in for a landing. It's not like any plane I've seen. It looks like a self-powered ultra-light. I can see the pilot's legs working some kind of pedals, but I can't see the pilot's face. The puzzle is missing a piece. I must have checked the package ten times and got down on the floor to feel around, but the piece is gone.

My brain feels thick and gluey as porridge. If Juan really did find a way into a magical faraway place, why would he send me the lock with the key missing? If I found the missing piece, would I find my way through? I press my face and body against the wall where Juan and I painted the mural and yell, "How do I find it?" The wall says nothing. No magic portal opens up. But I do feel something happen, as if the gluey porridge is draining from my brain and sweet clean water is rushing in. The water takes the form of words. *My puzzle island incomplete, then I see—the missing piece is . . .*

I grab a pen and paper. I don't want to lose the words. They come out like a flood of water, five syllables, then seven, then five.

*My puzzle island,*
*incomplete. Then I see—the*
*missing piece is . . . me.*

I don't know if it would make a bomb go off in Mr. Reid's head, but it sure makes one go off in mine. I run to the kitchen and grab Mom's basket full of craft paints and brushes. I go to work filling in the island that Juan left blank, the one surrounded by swirling grey mist. I paint a white sand beach, softly bending palm trees, a crowd of cheering people, and a self-powered aircraft coming in for a landing. Last of all, I paint in the pilot. I don't know how to make it look like me. I'm not the artist Juan is. I paint a head of black hair, small ears and a big smile. With a tiny brush, I paint on the name of the aircraft: *Nayl.*

# (Jewel)

When I was little, I had an imaginary friend named Sophie. She had loads of freckles and a gap between her front teeth, but in every other way she was just like me. She wanted to be a ballerina and a jockey and an astronaut. She liked barbecue chips and orange pop and sandwiches cut into triangles and stood on end like sailboats. She slept with me in my big double bed with my second-favorite doll, Penelope, tucked under her arm.

Mom says I'd tell anyone who listened about Sophie. But I can't talk about my new imaginary friend. You're not supposed to have imaginary friends if you're nineteen and reasonably bright and sane. And besides, she's not really imaginary. She's a flesh-and-blood person. It's our friendship that's imaginary.

I'm dreaming about her when Jake comes home, late as usual, close to midnight. What a beautiful dream. I'm dancing the tango by myself on a marble dance floor. I don't know where Jake is or why no one else is dancing. Maybe it's some kind of contest. I'm not nervous though. That's the nice thing about dreams. You can do things in them you can't do in real life. I'm dancing like I've never danced before! My body feels as light as air! My feet have wings! Then Diana starts dancing beside me with little Prince William in her arms, and I realize I'm holding Belle, and the four of us laugh and strut and whirl and spin. . . .

I feel Jake's rough stubble on my cheek before I can force my eyes open.

"Nice dream?" he whispers. "You were smiling."

I nod and kiss him. His lips taste of dust and salt. He looks down at Belle, who is beside me in a basket on the floor, smiling in her sleep.

"Maybe she's having the same dream you were," Jake whispers. Jake pulls off his paint-spattered sweat shirt and jeans and gives his right armpit a quick sniff.

"Can you stand me if I don't shower?" he asks. "I'm too tired, and I don't want to wake the baby."

I shake my head no and whisper, "Do that again."

"What, this?" He sniffs the other side, then flexes his biceps. I give him a sexy wink, but we both know we're just joking. It's too soon for that stuff. The doctor said to wait at least six weeks. Mom and Dad said to wait five years. The last thing we need is another baby. But part of me wants to do it all over again, this miraculous creation of life.

I clear the magazines I was reading off Jake's side of the bed so he can crawl in. Too late. I realize I forgot to hide the new issue of *Royalty*. I know Jake sees it. He doesn't say anything, but I see the look on his face. Imported glossy magazines aren't exactly in our budget right now.

I ask him about the house, our castle, we call it. Our little two bedroom castle with a leaky roof and damp basement and peeling walls, but Jake's fixing that. His boss said he'd rent it to us cheap if Jake fixed it up, so now he's killing himself working construction all day, rushing home for dinner and a quick play with Belle, then going to work on the castle till eleven or twelve at night.

He mutters something about plaster and wires and picking

something up on Friday, and I realize he's already half asleep. I have to hurry if I'm going to tell him about the fight.

"Jake? Mom and I had another . . . Jake?"

Too late. Jake can go from a standing position to REM sleep in thirty seconds flat. Oh well. I'll try to fall back asleep and tell my imaginary friend Diana about it. I turn off the lamp and lie back and watch the glow-in-the-dark stars on our ceiling fade, then disappear. I listen to the sound of breathing—Jake's and Belle's and mine—fill this dark basement bedroom in my parents' house. God, I hate living here. I appreciate it, but I hate it.

Mom looks like she's permanently wounded, as if my getting pregnant was something I did on purpose to bug her. And Dad walks around in shell shock, not sure whose side to take. He comes down to play with Belle. I know he loves her. I wish Mom did.

It takes a while to get back to sleep and when I do, I don't dream my lovely tango dream. I dream that Mom and I are lying on the backyard grass, watching for the first star. I'm a little kid again, I know, because I see how small my hands are when I reach up to pinch the first star between my fingers.

"Wish big, Little One!" Mom says in my dream. "Life holds such wonders for you!"

I ask for a story, and she tells me the one I love most, the one about their wedding stars, the two shooting stars that sizzled through the sky right after they said their vows in Gram and Gramps' garden. "Lucky, lucky, stars," Mom says. "We've been so happy. . . ."

Suddenly in my dream, I remember our fight.

"See!" I scream at her. I'm still beside her on the grass, but I'm grown up now. She looks at me as if she doesn't know me anymore. "You *were* happy!" I yell. *"You* were young and pregnant when *you* got married, and it didn't ruin *your* life!"

An explosion of light overhead obliterates the stars. It's the kitchen light, fluorescent and unforgiving. I'm counting butts in Mom's ashtray while she circles the table.

"I didn't have a choice, Jewel!" she spits. "You do!"

*Choice. Choice. Choice.* The word bounces around the kitchen, and everywhere it lands, I see a stain appear like a spreading inkblot until it forms the words of my mother's hidden message on the note stuck to the refrigerator, on the message board by the telephone, on the flowered wallpaper: Don't do what I did! DON'T DO WHAT I DID! *DON'T DO WHAT I DID!!*

Other familiar hated words escape from Mom's mouth like puffs of smoke: Abortion! Terminate! Not too late!

"Get out," I say to my mother.

"It's my house," she sneers.

I pick up her ashtray and smash it on the floor. Butts and ashes and shards of glass fly everywhere. Now it's Mom's face that is glass—one-way glass, a mirror.

I wake up, this time to the sounds of Belle snuffling and squeaking in the basket. I scoop her up and tiptoe into the rec room to nurse her.

"Dairy Bar's open for business, Piglet," I laugh. It's our private joke, mine and Belle's. I'm still amazed at how small and solid she is, and how fiercely I love her.

How could Mom have not wanted her to be born? To be scraped from my body and tossed out with the garbage?

*Choice.*

That hated word. I used to be pro-choice. I guess still am— for other people. But for me, the minute I found out I was pregnant, there was only one choice. Life.

There's not a sound from upstairs. It's 1:30 A.M. Mom and

Dad will be stretched out on opposite sides of their king-size bed, snoring a two-part harmony to "Strangers in the Night."

I use different tricks to stay awake while Belle eats. I show her the card the kids from the day care made for us. I tell her how they brought it with a mug full of jujubes and how devastated little Mitch was that Belle couldn't eat them because she has no teeth.

I tell her about the phone call from Kate today and how much she's liking university. Kate's nice to call. Funny, I used to have more friends than anyone at school, and now they hardly ever come around. It seemed the bigger my belly grew, the more they stayed away, as if what I had might be contagious. To be fair, Mandy and Alex still come around, but their eyes glaze over when I talk about feedings and burpings and diapers.

Maybe that's why I have imaginary conversations with the Princess of Wales, although since we've become such close imaginary friends, she insists that I call her Diana. I tell Belle what it's like in the palace, where little Wills lives. I imagine how we get together, the four of us, to sip tea and roll around on the carpets with our babies and discuss shades of poo. I'm sure Diana's eyes don't glaze over when Wills has weird-looking stuff in his diaper. I'm sure she gets just as scared as I do with Belle.

I tell Belle what Mom and Dad used to be like "BB," as Jake and I call it—"Before Baby," when things in the house were normal and civil and good, when no one was disappointed in anyone. That was Mom's word. She was disappointed in me.

"You're too young to start a family," she argued. "What about your plans for college?"

I told her that they'd always been more her plans than mine, that all I really wanted to do was be with kids. And not as an educator, a school principal or a curriculum maker. I want to be a mom. A wonderful, old-fashioned, stay-at-home, bake-cookies and play-in-the-sandbox mom. Call me a throwback, a dinosaur, a disgrace to my feminist foremothers, but it's what I want.

"There's more to being a mother than playing in a sandbox," she snapped. "And Jewel, you can be so much more!"

"What job could possibly be more important than raising a human being?" I said.

"You know what I meant."

"Mom, all my life you've been pushing me to be a doctor or a lawyer, like nothing else is good enough! Maybe I think *you* did a good job! Maybe I *admire* what you did. . . ."

"But I *did* go to college, Jewel! It took *years* of night school and *years* of hard work for your father and I to get where we are today. And it didn't have to be so hard, if only—"

"If only I hadn't been born."

That's what it always comes back to. The choice. If Mom could do it all over again, I wonder, what choice would she have made? What would she have done with the fetus that was me? Would she have let me live? Or would she have scraped me from her body and tossed me out with the garbage?

"I might not even be here now, Little One, and neither would you," I whisper to Belle. There's a lump in my throat the size of an orange, and my eyes are stinging with tears. I guess it comes with having a baby; your hormones get screwed up. I cry at the smallest things. Jake just laughs at me, but I never cry in front of Mom or Dad. I don't want them to think I'm anything but happy, serene and in control.

Belle is full of milk but wide awake—a real night owl. I sing some lullabies, then some old camp songs, but instead of falling asleep, she waves her arms and kicks her feet.

"You're a born dancer," I laugh. "Come on. I know what you'd like. But we have to be quiet."

Holding her close to my chest, I sneak up the stairs and down my parents' back hall to the heavy soundproof door that leads to Dad's Hideaway. It's what he calls his media room that he had built onto the back of the house last year. It's got black leather sofas slouching around a huge TV screen and shelves filled with his alphabetized record collection. At one end of the room, there's a glossy black piano and, at the other end, a polished oak dance floor with smoked mirrors on three sides. Mom and Dad used to win dance contests when they were young, just like Gram and Gramps, who still win contests at their retirement village in Florida.

We spent last New Year's Eve in this room, partying with Mom and Dad and Gram and Gramps. Ten months ago. So much has changed since then. We were supposed to go to Alex's party that night, but there was an awful snowstorm, so we stayed in. Jake made his famous Caesar salad and Gramps played the new piano and Dad made drinks from the cocktail cookbook Mom gave him for Christmas.

"What did you call that delightful beverage?" Gram slurred after downing three shooters in a row.

"A Slippery Nipple, Alice, and most women settle for a pair, but not you!"

Gram nearly fell off the couch laughing. Then she said, "The best antidote for pending drunkenness is dancing. A tango, Paul, if you please."

Then Dad put on "Hernando's Hideaway," and Jake started to look for a hiding place, but I said, "No, you don't! If you want to be part of this family, you have to learn how to tango."

It seems I was born knowing the tango. When I was little, Dad would spin me around the living room, holding me against his chest with my feet dangling. Later, I stood on his feet to learn the steps: *slow, slow, quick, quick, slow.* Jake was a bit clumsy.

"Don't worry," I told him. "It's like hockey. You have to practice."

The door clicks shut behind me, and for a moment we're plunged into darkness. Belle's breath comes faster. She cuddles into my chest. I feel for the light switch and turn on just one soft light. I flip through Dad's records and tell Belle how I used to come here and dance when she was inside me.

"Your favorite band was Genesis," I say, "but I think it's time for something different. Tonight, Piglet, I'll teach you to tango."

I find "Hernando's Hideaway" and place it on the record player. Then I get into position with Belle on the dance floor. She's looking up at me with her *what now?* expression.

"Watch my face, not my feet," I tell her. "Don't *think* about the music. *Feel* it. Your body will know what to do."

*Slow, slow, quick, quick, slow,* we dance to "Hernando's Hideaway." Belle relaxes into my chest, watching me, her lips forming a surprised "O!"

"I knew you'd like the tango," I whisper. When the song finishes, Belle's eyes are still wide open. Sleep is a long way off. We begin the next dance, a sad and smoky Bolero tango.

I don't hear Mom come into the room. I don't know she's there until she's right beside us on the dance floor. She's wearing her old terry robe, and her hair's sticking up all over. She smiles. I smile back, but I don't stop dancing. She touches Belle's velvet head, then moves behind us, puts her arms around us and picks up the dance, *slow, slow, quick, quick, slow,* both of us dancing the woman's part.

Until she says the words, I don't realize how much I longed to hear them.

"You are a good mother," she says and holds me as tight as I hold Belle, whose eyes are shining like two lucky stars that fell from the sky.

# (Tish)

Baba knew.

The newspapers said Alex was in the wrong place at the wrong time. They said no one could have saved her because no one could have known. But Baba knew.

Five whole minutes before the bullet left the gun, Baba knew what was going to happen, and, what's more, she told me. Somehow, somewhere in her poor tangled brain, she found the words to warn me, but I didn't understand what she said.

I replay those five minutes over and over again, thinking of ways I could have saved Alex, by running downstairs and pushing her out of the way or at least by yelling out the window. She might have pretended not to hear me and walked away, but at least she'd be gone from the path of the bullet.

Instead I did nothing, and because of that she is dead. My ex-best friend, Alex, is dead.

Alex saved *me* the day I met her.

It was my first day at a new school in a new town, and I was petrified. I leaned against the chain link fence wishing I could ooze through it and run home to Baba. Already I thought of her house as home. Money was tight after my parents' divorce, and Mom was holding down two jobs, so Baba was the one who got me ready for school, who braided my hair and stuffed me with pancakes for breakfast. Food meant love to Baba, and she gave me lots of both. That first day, she packed enough lunch for me to share with the whole class if I got up the nerve to offer it. So there I was at recess with a package of Baba's special Hairy Cookies in my pocket, gripping them so tightly some snapped between my fingers.

The playground was packed with kids who ignored me, so I ignored them and watched the one girl my age who wasn't skipping rope or playing tag. She was sitting farther down the fence, pretending to read, but really she was watching the other kids over the top of her book. Then she spotted me staring and came running over. Her dark curls bounced as she ran, and she grinned at me with perfectly small white teeth.

*Snap!* Another Hairy Cookie turned to dust in my pocket, but Alex didn't mind. She liked them, and she liked me, too. By the end of recess, she had declared Hairy Cookies her favorite food and me her best friend. It turned out that she was new, too, and said it was "density" that we found each other. She was in the other Grade Two class, but we played together at recess and after school. Baba let us hang around the kitchen while she made dinner, as long as we helped out.

"Many hands make light work!" she'd say, using one of the many sayings that were passed down like recipes from *her* grandmother, Baba Rose. That's who she got her sixth sense from, too. She used to amaze Alex by knowing who was calling when the phone rang, or what her Christmas presents were, even when we had disguised them with oddly shaped boxes. Alex and Mom both said she was psychic, but I had my doubts. Until now that is—and that time Alex fell off her bike.

We were riding home with our arms full of pussy willows, when Alex hit a stone and went flying. The whole length of her leg was scraped and bloody. She was crying and shaking and breathing funny.

"Tish, help me!" she whimpered.

I didn't know what to do except get her home fast to Baba, who was waiting for us at the door with a bowl of warm water and bandages as if she'd known Alex was hurt. She fixed up Alex's leg, and then wrapped her pillowy arms around her and rocked her back and forth, humming and patting her hair until Alex calmed down. We were getting too big for sitting on laps, but it seemed to be just what Alex needed.

Sometimes we went to Alex's house. It was enormous and new although it was made to look a hundred years old, with Victorian gingerbread dripping off the eaves and a round turret on one corner. Alex slept in the turret bedroom like a princess in a fairy-tale castle. We'd stretch out on her queen-size bed and talk for hours at a time about everyone and everything. We'd gossip about our teachers, pick apart our classmates and dream out loud. Her mom would bring us fancy store-bought cookies on a tray, and her dad, Dr. Meyers, would call me their Kid Number Two.

Alex had all twenty of her Barbies displayed in a glass cabinet. She said she got her first Barbie when she was three and insisted on getting a Ken so they could have weddings. I was glad she was past playing with Barbies. I never liked the way they had to totter around on high heels because their feet were shaped that way. The most fun I had with my Barbie was feeding her to my toy crocodile. Not that I told Alex about that.

In Grade Seven, Alex started plastering her walls with posters of guys who had square jaws and smoldering eyes and locks of hair drooping down their foreheads. Every few months she'd fall in love with a different movie star and describe to me in detail her fantasies, which always ended with a crushing passionate kiss.

She never understood why I didn't love those guys, too. They're not real, I'd tell her. They look like they're molded from plastic, like Barbie's Ken.

In high school, the posters came down, but the crushes continued, on real guys this time. Grade Thirteen guys who were on the football team. Alex would get all flustered and silly if one of them walked by or held a door open for us.

She worried that someday she'd get asked out and not be ready.

"Ready for what?" I wanted to know.

"For kissing," said Alex. "I need to practice."

"You mean like on the back of your hand or something?"

"No. . . ." She giggled. "What if *we* practiced, you and me? Then we'll both be ready."

I didn't want to, but I couldn't tell her why.

Alex shrugged. "Okay, it's no big deal."

But it *was* a big deal, for me. I told her I'd think about it.

Two days later, we were in her turret bedroom when I said I'd do it. I've never been so nervous. Alex just laughed, as if it meant nothing to her.

"Close your eyes so you can pretend I'm a guy," she said. "And tilt to the right, okay?"

They were little kisses, tilted to the right at first, then straight on, then to the left. Her lips were soft as feathers. Our noses rubbed. I felt like a blind person discovering for the first time what my best friend looked like. We kissed some more. In her mind, Alex was probably seeing a Grade Thirteen football stud or maybe a square-jawed movie star. But I was thinking, *Wow! This is Alex! Beautiful, special, amazing Alex!*

She jerked her head back. Her face was flushed pink.

"Alex, what's wrong?"

"I can't do it!" she said. "I pretended at first but then . . . ew-w-w-w! It was too gross!" She made a face, wiped her mouth and laughed. "Let's forget we did that, okay, Tish?"

"Sure," I said.

I stayed a bit longer. We looked at some magazines, and then I went home. Same as always, except now it was different. Now I knew I loved Alex, and she knew it, too.

That was two years ago, when we were fifteen. That spring, Keenan Jones asked Alex to go to the formal. He wasn't in Grade Thirteen, but he did play football and Alex said he was the best-looking guy in Grade Twelve. I didn't go. I hated the dances, where people would either make out in the corners of the gym or stand by the stage like zombies and watch the band.

But all Alex talked about was going to the formal. And after the formal, all she talked about was Keenan. Keenan this and Keenan that. When we talked in the hall at school, she'd always be glancing over my shoulder to see if he was coming. Soon she was busy all the time with Keenan and his friends, a tight little group of cheerleader girls and jock guys. They even let Alex onto the cheerleading team as a spare, even though the tryouts had been months before.

The worst part was that she seemed to love it, love *them,* the same people we used to pick apart in her room, the same people we used to call shallow, boring, snobbish airheads. To be fair, she did try to include me. She'd try to coax me to go with them to movies or to their field parties, but I kept making excuses not to go.

The one thing I did agree to do was the mock royal wedding at school last year. Alex was Princess Anne, and she got me the part of a bridesmaid. I did it because I wanted to be with Alex, but I hated the itchy dress and the way they pulled my hair back so I looked like a horse and the way everyone acted like someone they weren't. I didn't get to be much with Alex anyway. I was stuck helping Mandy Solesby, the other bridesmaid, arrange

Jewel's train and stopping the flower girls from rolling all over it. I should have backed out and let someone else have the part, but I didn't, and my scowling face is recorded forever in the official royal wedding portrait in the '82 yearbook. A horse among beauty queens. The troll at Ken and Barbie's wedding.

Things were never the same after that kiss in her bedroom. We never talked about it, but I thought about it all the time. It used to be Alex always daydreaming, and now it was me. My daydream about Alex started the same way it had in real life, in her turret bedroom, a smile on her lips, her head tilted to the right, but instead of ending in revulsion and rejection, it ended with acceptance and understanding. I've dreamed this scene so many times that I can almost believe it's a real memory.

A few months ago, in May, I wrote Alex a letter and mailed it to her gingerbread house. I remember every word.

*Dear Alex,*

*Every time I try to talk to you, I turn into a witch. I'm sorry. Maybe I can say what needs to be said better on paper. I'll try anyway.*

*I've been feeling so many things lately. Anger, confusion, but mostly sadness. I miss you. Can you say that to a friend, a girl friend? Well, I do miss you. I miss the friendship we had, and I'm sorry if I did something to destroy it.*

*I'm glad you've found Keenan. It seems for as long as I've known you, you've longed to fall in love. I hope he's everything you wished for.*

*You're probably wondering what the point of this letter is. I guess it's this . . . that I've watched our friendship fade during the past year or so and yet we've never talked about it. Maybe if we stop pretending we're still friends, I'll stop being mad at you and myself. I want you to remember me*

*as I used to be, and not like the witch I've become. So I'm
writing to say good-bye. Our friendship deserves at least
that—a decent burial.*

    *So farewell, my best and dearest friend,*
                       *Tish*

I mailed the letter on a Friday afternoon and spent the
whole weekend wondering how to break into the mailbox so I
could get it back. What had I been thinking? I didn't want to
end our friendship! If it was possible at all to save it, I was willing.

I couldn't face her. I faked the flu on Monday and Tuesday,
and by the time I went back to school on Wednesday, Alex had
received the letter. I knew it as soon as I saw her face. She was in
the bathroom putting on lipstick and nearly dropped the tube
when she saw me.

"Tish! Hi . . . how are you feeling?"

*Like I've made the biggest mistake of my life.* "Better, thanks."

"You had that flu that's going around, eh?"

I nodded.

"I was going to call. . . ." said Alex.

*But you didn't.*

"I . . . uh," she glanced around and crouched down to look
under the stall doors to make sure we were alone, "I got your letter."

"Alex—"

"It was amazing, Tish. I'm so glad you sent it."

"You are?"

"I've been feeling bad about what's happened, too. Things
aren't the same as they used to be, are they?"

"Well, no. . . ."

"So I was thinking, maybe you're right. Maybe we should take
a break for a while."

"Oh . . ." What was wrong with me? I wanted to grab her by

the shoulders and say, *Forget the stupid letter! I take it back! I'll be nice, I'll play along, I'll go to those stupid parties and find a boyfriend if that's what you want!* But I didn't really want those things. I wanted Alex and our friendship back, the way it used to be.

"Okay, I guess that's best," I said.

Alex smiled, and I remembered her perfect small white teeth on the playground that first day.

"See ya around, Tish."

"Yeah, see ya."

Alex dropped the lipstick tube into her purse, walked out of the bathroom and out of my life. The bell rang. History class was starting, but I didn't care. I sat in a stall and thought about the word *dump*. I'd been *dumped*. *Dumped* where people *dump*.

It stank in the bathroom. I hadn't noticed it before, but I sure noticed it now, a rotten, wet, putrid smell that reached into my stomach, churned up my breakfast and made me throw up. Again and again, I retched in the toilet until my eyes watered and my throat burned and there was nothing left inside me.

When the trembling stopped, I rinsed my mouth, splashed cold water on my face and walked to class, convinced that I'd ended what had already been ending and that now I could get over Alex and let the place inside where I kept my feelings for her grow cold and hard.


In October, a film crew descended on our town to shoot some scenes for a suspense thriller called *You Never Know*. All everyone talked about that week was the star, Oksana Riker—where she'd been seen around town, how nice she was to the groupies who followed her everywhere. We were let out of school early on

Friday to watch the filming. It was a foot-chase scene down Main Street, so Baba and I had front-row seats upstairs in her enclosed sun porch, where Alex and I used to watch the Santa Claus parade every year.

I could see Alex on the sidewalk below, pressing against the traffic barriers, laughing and tossing her hair the way she used to when she was trying to catch a guy's eye. Maybe she was hoping to get discovered by someone on the film crew. She'd always wanted to be an actress.

Margaret, Baba's lady-sitter, came in to say good-bye, and Baba gave her a long tight hug. Sometimes Baba thinks Margaret is her mother and cries when she has to go.

Baba had arranged my old stuffed animals beside her on the couch so they could watch TV with us. She had her feet on the coffee table, and I was painting her toenails bubblegum pink. The color wasn't my choice.

"Are you sure, Baba?" I asked when she pointed to the pink bottle. "That one's kind of gaudy."

"Yup," she said. That's all she said anymore—"yup," "nope," or she'd shrug her shoulders to say, "I don't know." I hadn't heard a full sentence cross her lips in ages.

I chattered away as I painted her nails, telling her about the film shoot and glancing out the window now and then.

"Alex is down there," I said.

Baba's foot jerked suddenly and wound up with a pink stripe painted down her big toe. She sat up straight as a board, eyes wide with panic, her mouth opening and closing like a fish gasping for air.

"Baba! What is it?"

I wished I had her sixth sense so I could read her mind. She was trying so hard to tell me something. Finally the words came out, croaky and small, but lined up in the right order, a real sentence: "You . . . never know . . . from where you sit . . . where the man . . . in the balcony . . . will spit."

It was a miracle! I glanced up at the picture of Jesus that hangs over Baba's TV. Over the years, I'd heard dozens of Baba's proverbs and sayings, but I'd never heard that one.

"Can you say it again, Baba?"

She shook her head, and tears filled her eyes as she rocked back and forth on the couch. The stuffed animals wedged around her tumbled to the floor. I wrapped my arms around her and rocked with her, humming the tuneless song she used to sing to me. When she calmed down, she said it again. "You never know, you never know, from where you sit . . . where the man in the balcony will spit!"

"Are you talking about yourself, Baba?" I thought maybe she meant God, up in heaven, was spitting on her by giving her Alzheimer's. But she shook her head.

"About *me* then? Are you talking about *me?*" I had told her about my feelings for Alex, but mostly because I thought she couldn't understand.

"Nope," said Baba.

"Well, *who* then?"

"You never know!" she said. Then she clamped her mouth shut and began rocking again. I held her and hummed and thought about what she had said.

*You never know from where you sit where the man in the balcony will spit.*

Right on, Baba, I thought. Spit happens. Spit rains down on you. Alex was my best friend, and now she's lined up with the other spitters, her stupid quarterback boyfriend and her airhead cheerleader friends, spitting. Give me a T! Give me an I! Give me an S! Give me an H! What does that spell? FREAK!

The word echoed in my head like a gunshot. *Freak! Freak!* But it wasn't an echo. It *was* a gunshot. Baba whimpered.

"It's okay. It's just the film shoot," I told her, but I looked out the window to make sure. There was an awful lot of screaming suddenly, right outside our house.

If I'd been down in the crowd, I never would have seen Alex on the ground with all those people pressing around her. But high up as I was, I could see her eyes flutter open and shut. I could see her lips moving, trying to speak. I could see the patch of pavement beneath her head become a dark wet halo.

I had a front-row balcony seat for The Death of Alex.

Beautiful, special, amazing Alex.

My ex–best friend, Alex.


I read about Timothy Horn in the newspapers. Age nineteen, author of eight hundred love letters to Oksana Riker. He had hitchhiked all the way from his home near Detroit to see her. In Levis and a navy coat, he looked like everyone else in the crowd, and that's why no one noticed him until he climbed to the roof of the Sub Shop across from our house, pulled a gun from his pocket and fired three shots at Oksana. The first two hit the pavement. The third one hit Alex.

I watched her die as one last shot rang out. I didn't hear, notice or care about it, but I read about it after. Just before the police rushed out on the roof to grab him, Timothy Horn shot himself. *Freak.*

I spend a lot of time hating Timothy Horn. I hate that he was born. I hate that his father had a gun that was easy to steal. I hate that he was a bad shot. I hate his obsession, which reminds me of mine.

If Baba were herself, she'd say, "Let go of the hate. Forgive him." I can't. He took something from me that I thought I'd already lost. But she was still there inside me, and he killed her. The cold hard place inside me ached. There was a hole in it now, with bloody ragged edges, as if a bullet had torn its way through.

Mom couldn't get time off work, so I went by myself to Alex's funeral. The church was packed. I sat in the back pew beside Ginger Byam, who's in my Family Studies class. I wondered what she was doing there. She was a loner and had never been Alex's friend as far as I knew.

"What's in the basket?" she whispered.

"Babka," I whispered back. When she looked confused, I added, "Cake for the reception. Alex liked it."

Then we stopped talking because Mandy Solesby had stood up at the front. I remembered that she was the minister's daughter. I'd always thought of her as just one of the cheerleaders in a tight sweater and short skirt, giggling about nothing. But this was a Mandy I'd never seen in school. She read a poem about friendship and talked about what Alex's friendship had meant to her. Mandy's voice quavered, but she never lost it. I glanced at Ginger. I could tell she was impressed, too.

At the reception afterward, I placed the babka on the food table with one of Baba's embroidered napkins fanned beneath it. "Presentation is important," Alex used to say. I wanted to talk to her parents, but they were always surrounded by family or Keenan and his friends, and I just couldn't face them.

I wandered over to the picture wall, where there were snapshots of Alex. I was in some of them, swimming in their pool, roasting hot dogs at their family barbecues, lying beside Alex in a pile of leaves with only our faces showing.

There were some recent pictures of Alex that were beautiful. Sweaty and smiling after a cheerleading practice, soft and serious against a backdrop of pussy willows and a close-up that showed her laughing eyes and perfect white teeth.

"I guess you knew she wanted to be a model, eh?" Ginger had come up beside me to look at the pictures, too.

I nodded. "She could have been one easily. Look at these."

"I don't have to," said Ginger. "I took them."

"Really?" Then I remembered it was Ginger who took the royal wedding portraits, where we all look so stiff, but Alex looked so natural in these photos. So alive. "Could I get a copy of this one?" I asked.

"Sure," she said. "You guys were best friends, weren't you?"

"Once upon a time we were."

"She talked about you the day I took these by the pussy willows. She told me about falling off her bike . . . when you helped her."

"She was always helping Alex, weren't you Tish?" I turned to see Alex's parents, holding hands behind me. The mascara was smudged beneath her mother's eyes. Her dad winked at me like he used to. "Hi, Number Two," he said.

I didn't know if Alex had told them why we drifted apart. I didn't know if they'd seen the letter.

"I miss her so much," I whispered.

Mrs. Meyers nodded and put her hand to her lips. "Here I go crying all over again."

"I'm sorry," I said. What I meant was, I'm sorry I didn't understand Baba's warning. I'm sorry I didn't save your daughter. I'm so sorry.


I left quickly so I wouldn't have to talk to anyone else, ran down the church steps and headed up the street, cursing my stupid dress shoes. I felt like kicking them off so I could run faster and let the sidewalk rip open the soles of my feet. I wanted to bleed, and I wanted Baba to fix it. I wanted her to wrap her pillowy arms around me and rock and hum and pat my hair. I wanted her to tell me something, anything, even another cryptic proverb that might help me get through this.

"Tish! Wait up!" Keenan ran up beside me. "I tried to find you in there, but you got away."

*It's called avoiding you,* I thought. Then I saw he'd been crying.

Poor Keenan. I'd spent a lot of time hating him before I started hating Timothy Horn. *Say something,* I told myself. *Be polite. He just lost his girlfriend.*

"Keenan . . . I'm sorry about Alex." How many times had I said that today or had it said to me?

"Thanks, Tish. Same to you. I—uh—wanted to ask you . . ." He looked as awkward as I felt.

"A few of us are getting together at my place after this, to talk about Alex and stuff. Would you come?"

"Oh, I don't think so . . . but thanks for asking."

"Tish? Please come. You were Alex's . . . best friend."

I looked him right in the eye then, and I saw something there. He *knew.* Alex must have told him about the kiss and the letter, about my feelings for her. Oh God. I wanted to sink through the sidewalk.

But then I realized something else. He knew, but he still wanted me to come. And I realized that of all the people in the world, maybe only Keenan could understand how I felt, because he had loved her, too.

Margaret was home with Baba making Hairy Cookies for tonight's dessert. Baba was probably fine, happy with the woman she thought was her mother. There would be time later to sit with her and hum and rock and tell her about Alex's funeral.

"Okay," I said to Keenan. "I'll come."

## rabbits

# (Derek)

It's shaping up to be a good party. The girls are hot, the guys are cool, my parents are five hundred miles away and I just know it's going to be a wicked night.

Most of my new team, the Icemen, are here with their girl friends, who happen to be the best-looking bunch of rink babes I've ever seen. A few of the guys from my old team, the Lions, are here, too. And Molly Freestone showed up with her "ladies-in-waiting." I didn't invite them, but those girls can sniff out a party a mile away. I could hardly turf them out after Molly laid a hello kiss on me that got both teams cheering. Not that it meant anything. It's just Molly's way, but, still, it's probably best that Laura didn't see it.

Laura's the reason I've been hanging out here on the landing. I'm trying not to look overanxious, but I want to grab the door when she comes. She's not used to this crowd. I wonder what she'll think of them, and what they'll think of her. I haven't felt this nervous since . . . well, since Ginger.

Laura's not like Ginger. She's not like Molly. She's not like any girl I've known. Things that work on other girls don't work on Laura, like this great evening I had planned. I was going to pick her up in Dad's Corvette and bring her here for a romantic pre-party dinner. I was even going to cook, and I've never cooked for anyone before, let alone a vegetarian!

After dinner, I was hoping to show her my new waterbed. If she seemed uncomfortable, I was going to tell her what I told my parents—that I needed a warm waterbed to soothe my sore muscles after a game. So they bought it for me as a reward for scoring three goals in my first game as an Iceman.

My brothers weren't fooled, though, when they came by last week to check it out. Jeff said, "So basically what you've got is another trophy for your collection, except this one's big enough to roll around in with a girl." Mike and Joe stuck a sign on the headboard that said YIELD! STUD ON BOARD! My brothers give me a hard time about being spoiled, but I'm pretty sure they're proud of me. Any one of them would have gladly slept on a park bench to have had the chance to play Junior A, let alone score a hat trick the first night. So I figure I'm not just playing for myself. I'm playing for all of them.

Anyway, Laura wouldn't let me pick her up. She preempted me for some radio science show that she said she couldn't miss. I even offered to pick her up later, even though the party would have started, but no, she wanted to walk. In fifteen-below weather, she wanted to walk!

So much for dinner. So much for the tour of my waterbed. So much for finding out how soothing Laura's skin would have felt against mine after a hard day getting ready for this party.

I know I've got to check those thoughts (stuff them in the penalty box, two minutes for lusting!) because coming on strong and fast works on the ice, but it doesn't work on certain girls. And Laura is special. I don't want to blow it.

The coach says playing against certain teams is like watching reruns of old TV shows. The guys' moves are so predictable it almost takes the fun out of winning. You relax, get lazy. A guy you've never seen before skates out for the face-off, but you figure he's nothing to worry about. He's a shrimp with a pasty face and watery eyes, the type of guy you just have to stare down to let him know the puck has your name on it. But while you're busy staring, the shrimp takes off with the puck.

Laura's a bit like that, full of surprises. I guess she was there for years, sitting at the front of the class with the rest of the brains. I didn't think she was particularly shy or stuck up or anything. I just didn't think about her. But one day I was griping about all the book reports we have to do, and she handed me a little book called *Jonathan Livingston Seagull.*

"It's a fast read," she said, "and a good story."

She was right. I read the whole thing. It's about a seagull who always wants to fly higher, faster and better—which is kind of how I feel about hockey. I got an A on that book report. So I asked Laura if she knew any more good short books, and she said to stop by her house that night.

When she answered the door, my jaw must have dropped six inches. She'd been working out, I guess, because she was kind of sweaty and she was wearing a skintight leotard thing that dancers wear, and oh man, she had a knockout body! I had no idea what she'd been hiding under those long skirts and sweaters that she usually wears. Then she apologized and said she forgot I was coming over, and I think she really meant it. Most girls spend a long time getting ready before I come over, I know, because they say things like, "Do you like my hair this way? It took forever to do." And about three cans of hair spray from the looks of it. I never touch that kind of hair. I'd be worried my hand would get stuck in it, and I'd have to skate down the ice, dragging the girl's head like a bowling ball, while my parents holler from the seats, "Don't let her slow you down!"

Laura's hair is poker straight and hangs past her waist. A few more inches and she wouldn't need to wear clothes. Just hair. Beautiful silky hair a guy could get lost in. Light brown with streaks of gold running through it. Her eyes are golden, too. They're usually hiding behind her glasses, but when she took them off the other day to wipe them, wham! It was like falling into a keg of cool amber beer when you're dying of thirst.

While I stood there like an idiot, Laura invited me in and offered me some little round things in a pottery bowl.

"Uh, what are they?" I asked.

"Chick-peas," she laughed. "But I call them Little Bums."

Good thing I was sitting down by then, because when a sexy girl starts talking sexy, certain parts of me stand at attention. She didn't seem to realize she was talking sexy. She wasn't nervous or giggly, either. She just walked around, picking up a book here and there from the stacks that were on just about every chair, table and footstool in the room, except the one I was sitting on. I watched her perfect ass, firm and round as a chick pea, as she reached to get a book off a shelf.

"So do you have a boyfriend?" I asked. A girl this great must have some university guy stashed away in the city.

She turned and looked surprised. I'm not positive, but I think she was changing her mind about me from "jock" to "potential date." It was a new experience for me—to be checked over, assessed—and I found that sexy, too. I had to think fast, say something to make her want me.

"You're an iceberg, Laura."

"You mean . . . I'm cold?"

"No! I mean, you're full of surprises. Like in school, you're just showing a little tip of yourself—and a nice tip it is, too. . . ."

She smiled.

"But I bet there's a lot more below the surface."

She didn't say anything for a minute, and I started to get nervous, but I kept smiling as if everything was cool. Finally she smiled back, and that's when I noticed that her mouth is shaped like a heart. Her lips go up from the middle, then down and then up again at the corners. Some girls draw on that shape with lipstick, but on Laura it's all natural and full of secrets that I'm dying to find out.

An hour later I'm still partying on the landing by the door. I've got friends jammed around me, an almost finished beer in one hand and a fresh one in the other. I'm feeling much more relaxed. It's an awesome party. My friends are great. Laura will love them.

The doorbell rings and it's Jake, my best buddy the last couple of years. We used to play on the Lions together, take the same classes at school. Sometimes we'd skip off and head to the racetrack.

"Good to see ya, man! Where's Jewel?"

"Home with Belle," says Jake. "We couldn't get a baby-sitter."

We all kind of laugh because Jewel used to baby-sit everyone else's little brothers and sisters. Now they've got Belle, who'd be about two months old now. I still can't believe it, the Jakester . . . a dad! Pulled off course in the prime of life. I heard somewhere that guys peak at eighteen, and here Jake's already tied to one girl and probably too tired to do it half the time anyway.

Jake and Jewel brought the baby to see one of my games this fall. I guess I should be flattered. They don't get many nights out, and she's a cute kid—if you don't mind snot and slobber—but she sure cramps their social life. Just a year ago, Jake never missed a party, and now he misses them all and hockey, too! For the first time since he was a kid, Jake's not playing hockey. He's all work, work, work . . . and baby-sitting.

I guess the nice thing to do would be to tell Jake to call Jewel and get her to come over, baby and all, but I can't bring myself to do it. Babies at a party are definitely uncool.

Jake lets me off the hook. "Jewel couldn't have come anyway. She was too tired. Belle was fussing all day 'cause—"

"You look like shit, too," I say.

Jake laughs and throws his coat on the rack that looks ready to crash at any second. He leans back against it as Molly squeezes between us.

"Jake! You've got dark circles under your eyes," she purrs. "Jewel not taking care of you?"

"No, Jewel's great. The best." Then he explains that he's tired because after his paying job is done for the day, he goes and works on the rental house they're renovating. Somewhere between the joists and the drywall, he loses me.

"Whoa there, buddy! Jake, as your friend, I've got to warn you, you're getting *boring*. You made it to a party. Remember, *parties?* Now get in there, get yourself a drink, or better yet, get drunk and have a good time!"

While I'm giving him the lecture, Molly gives Jake one of her hello kisses that lasts about a minute. Jake's eyes bug out at me while she's doing it. At least he looks wide awake now.

Two of the scarier Icemen, Ivan and Tipp, start clapping and hooting like gorillas. The rest of the crowd on the stairs joins in. "Oo-oo-oo-oo!" Jake pushes Molly back, but not in an unfriendly way, and bows to the hooting crowd. He holds up his hands as if to say, *I give up; I'm gonna enjoy my night out.* Then he follows Molly down to the rec room, where the sweet smell of hash is rising up like steam from a sweaty head.


Pulled off course. My parents talk a lot about my *course.* Following it. Staying on it. Not getting pulled off it.

They think Ginger pulled me off course a couple of years ago. Mom swears that's how I hurt my ankle—I was paying more attention to Ginger than I was to the game. Ginger was . . . my first. My first kiss, my first girl friend, my first love . . . *Whatever that means,* as Prince Charles would say.

I feel I almost know Prince Charles, since I had to play him in the mock royal wedding last year. To be fair the part should have gone to an older guy, but Miss Twitchit's always had a soft spot for me. She practically begged me to do it. "We need a tall, dark, handsome prince who has the manners of a gentleman. That's you to a tee, Derek," she said. I wonder what she'd say to the belch I let fly a minute ago?!

My parents hated me doing the royal wedding. They said it pulled me off course just like Ginger did. As far as they're concerned, the only right course for me is hockey. Dad says I've got talent most guys would kill for. He says if I can stay off the injured list and apply myself, I could go all the way to the NHL.

Some days I see it like I'm seeing the future—me in Maple Leaf Gardens, standing proud and tall while they play the national anthem. And those days I try hard. I skate hard. I play hard. Nothing can stop me.

But other days I feel something like a tap on my shoulder, a tug in another direction, and I wonder if there's something else I'm meant to do—maybe something I'm not so good at, but something I'd really love doing. Those days, I can't see the future, and the magic doesn't happen on the ice. Those days, Dad won't even talk to me, he's so mad.

I've got to admit, for the past week, Laura's been pulling me off course. I don't know what it is about her. She hasn't even been to one of my games. But there's something. . . .

I used the bathroom when I was at her house the other night. There was a book on the back of the toilet tank that I know was hers; her name was inside along with a drawing of a head with a heart inside it, and inside the heart was a brain, and inside the brain was the word *love.* The face looked like Laura's. The book was about parallel universes. Now, what kind of girl reads about parallel universes while she's going to the can? I guess the kind of girl I'm falling in love with does . . . whatever that means.

*Here's to brother Derek, brother Derek, brother Derek,*
*Here's to brother Derek, he's with us tonight!*
*So drink chugga-lugga, drink chugga-lugga,*
*drink chugga-lugga, drink chugga-lugga,*
*Here's to brother Derek, he's with us tonight!*

Glad to oblige, I chug down my beer. My fifth. Or is it my sixth? It doesn't matter. What matters is I feel good. I lick my lips, raise my bottle high and let loose a king-size belch just as the doorbell rings again.

This time it's Laura. Wow, is it Laura! Looking like an angel with snowflakes on her hair. She smiles with those amazing heart-shaped lips, takes off her glasses to wipe them, and I am gone, falling headfirst into those deep amber eyes. I don't even try to resist this time. I just grab her and kiss her. She tenses up and I force myself to stop. No sense blowing it in the first five minutes.

"Sorry," I whisper into her soft hair, "but you're irresistible."

Is it the red spotlight on the lawn, or is she actually blushing? I think she is! She's flattered! Confidence surges inside me. It's going to happen. A breakaway. I'm flying down the ice, and nothing can stop me from scoring.

I add her coat to the heap and put my arm around her shoulders. She feels so good. Her sweater's made of something silky, and the color is better than brown. It's like creamy Easter chocolate, so rich it'll make you sick if you eat too much. Her skirt's the same color, but a different material—that gauzy stuff you can almost see through. I wish I could get a better look. Maybe later. . . . Right now it's time to show her around and show her off, my beautiful one-of-a-kind Laura.

At first it's fantastic. Laura's a big hit. We work our way

through the rec room. Laura says the right kinds of things. She asks people questions about what they love most, and with this crowd, it's usually hockey. It turns out Laura knows more about hockey than I thought. I'm loving her more every minute.

Finally we reach the bar so I can get her a drink. I ask her what vegetarians are allowed to drink and she laughs. "Well, they let us drink wine. Made from grapes, you know."

Behind the bar our fingers touch when I hand her the glass. Her fingers are soft, too. *Is every inch of this girl soft?* I wonder. Suddenly a big guy with an even bigger nose butts his face into our space. It's Russ, captain of the Icemen. I'm nice to him because I have to be, but I don't really like him. The next second I start liking him a lot less. He's leaning over the bar, grinning at my girl.

"Hey, good-lookin'! Can you give me an orgasm?"

It's as plain as the crooked nose on his ugly face that he's not talking about the drink. I'm gearing up to smash him one when Laura, calm as anything, says, "I've never made one, but I'm willing to try. What's in it? Vodka?"

And just like that, my temper cools off. I can't believe I was about to hit the captain. Laura's good for me! How excellent is that? It's like finding out that Cheezies are a health food. I pass Russ a beer and tell him to go look for orgasms somewhere else.

"Sorry," I whisper to Laura. "He can be a jerk."

"It's okay. Let me guess, he plays offense."

"Yeah, how'd you know?" Then I get the joke and laugh. Wow. A beautiful sexy girl who makes hockey jokes. This is my lucky life.

"So you didn't tell me how your walk was, Laura. Did you freeze?"

"Oh no. It was perfect. Magical. Right at the end of your street the most incredible thing happened—"

Someone else comes up asking for wine. If we weren't back here, people would just help themselves. I pour the wine, then grab Laura's hand. "Come on, Laur, let's get out of here."

We work our way through the crowd to the loveseat in the corner. I look into her golden eyes. "Now tell me what happened," I say.

I don't know what I expected. I thought maybe she found money or something. But it turns out that the wonderful thing was a couple of rabbits who let her pet them. Wild rabbits, she says. Big deal, right? But Laura's so excited about it, and her eyes sparkle so much when she tells me, I can't help but get excited, too. Parts of me get really, really excited. Maybe it's because of her fresh-air smell. Maybe it's because her heart-shaped mouth is finally spilling a secret.

"I had a pet rabbit when I was a kid," I tell her and realize too late it wasn't the best subject to bring up. The rabbit died. I was too rough playing with it. I even dropped it once. Poor stupid rabbit. I'd wanted a dog anyway.

"Isn't this great?" I say. "Just the two of us . . . in a roomful of people?"

She won't be distracted. "You had a rabbit? I didn't think you were the bunny type. What did you call him?"

I haven't a clue. "Peter," I say.

"Like Peter Rabbit?"

I nod.

"Oh, I love that!" she says.

Actually, I said "Peter" because my buddy Pete Grummond just walked by, but the name seemed to score major points with Laura.

We talk some more. Then suddenly the music stops, and they call me across the room to fix the tape player. I groan. Next time I try to get close to a girl, it won't be at a party of mine. Laura stays put to talk to one of the Icemen's girl friends who says she just has to know if Laura's hair color is natural. "Whoa, girl stuff. I'm outta here!" I say, but I wink at Laura. "I'll be back soon, gorgeous."

It doesn't take me long to fix the stereo, but it takes awhile to work my way back to Laura. People I haven't talked to yet keep grabbing me, and it would be rude to walk away just as they're telling me how well I'm playing this year. Besides, from what I can see, Laura's doing great on her own. I like that she doesn't need to be stuck to me every minute of the party. And I like watching her through the crowd, knowing she's mine. I'm watching when Molly sidles up to her. A face-off. Laura must know that Molly and I used to go out, but she's clearly not going to let Molly intimidate her. I'm proud of Laura for not backing down. A picture pops into my head of the two of them mud wrestling for the Grand Prize—me!

Molly disappears into the crowd, then shows up a few minutes later, plastered to my side. "Derek, I was bad earlier," she whispers in my ear. "I went into your room to see your new waterbed, and it got me so, well, you know how warm it is and wet. . . ." Like her mouth on my ear. I wish she wouldn't do that. She knows my weak spots. "I left you a note under the covers," she whispers.

"Jeezuz, Moll—"

"I know it was dumb, but I didn't know you had a date tonight! Who would have thought? You and . . . well, anyway. Don't worry. I'll get rid of the note." She looks like a kitten when she's saying sorry. I can't stay mad.

But I realize I better get back to Laura. Maybe it's time we found a quieter spot. Maybe it's time to show her my room. . . .

Laura looks different by the time I get back to her. Not all soft, like before. I see hard edges now.

"Hey, gorgeous! You okay? Did—uh—someone say something?"

"Well, you've been gone for an hour. A lot of people said a lot of things."

An alarm starts going off in my head. Bitch alert! I hate girls who play head games, who figure you should know what's bugging them, as if you're psychic or something.

But Laura's straightforward. She says she's mad and why.

"Derek, it's not you. I've spent the last twenty minutes discussing the virtues of hair removal by wax, razor or tweezer, and the twenty minutes before that arguing with a couple of your team-mates about the insane salaries professional hockey players make."

She was arguing with my teammates about NHL salaries? Is she out of her freaking *mind?*

"Uh—who were you talking to?"

"I think their names are Ivan and Tipp."

"Oh great. Ivan the Terrible and Tipp the Scales."

Laura laughs. She doesn't know how bad this is. I don't know them well, but well enough to know they're nuts. They'd fight an ant if it complained while they were stomping on it. I look around, but I don't see them.

"They left to get some subs," Laura says. "They were taking orders. Didn't they get over to your side of the room?"

"No."

"I hope you're not upset, Derek."

"No."

"Good, because I wasn't obnoxious. I just stated my opinion. They got a bit excited, but I smoothed it over. You're not the only one who can be charming, you know."

"You certainly are that," I smile. "I wish I'd known they were going. I could use a sub."

"I'll share mine. They're getting me a veggie sub."

"You *told* them you're a vegetarian?"

"Yes. . . ." She goes stiff, as if someone just ran a finger up her back. "Is there something wrong with that?"

"No. . . ." *Yes!* Before every game, these guys eat a pound of steak so rare it's almost breathing. They call the rest of us girls for eating pasta on game nights.

"I . . . think I better go, Derek."

"No! Don't go."

"I might ruin your reputation with the guys."

"It's not a problem, really."

"I need some air anyway."

I follow her up the stairs to the landing. I know if I don't do something soon, she'll walk out of the front door and never come back.

"Laura," I whisper into the silky hair that covers her ear. "There's a place where you can get some air. Where we can be alone for a while."

She lets me take her up to my room. A few people snicker as we pass through the crowd in the living room and the lineup outside the bathroom. Laura doesn't flinch. She walks as straight and tall as a queen, and I find myself wondering why she wasn't in the mock royal wedding last year. Jewel made a great Princess Di, but Laura . . . I don't know why I never thought of it before. She has it all—beauty, brains, charm and, what do they call it . . . poise? Yeah. Then I'm alone in my room with all that beauty, brains, charm and poise, and it takes all my self-control not to grab her right away. I sit on the edge of the waterbed and watch her stroll around my room, looking at the pictures and trophies. It reminds me of being at her house, watching her. That night, I checked out her room without her knowing it. Now she's checking out mine, while I watch. It's a sexy thing. She touches my MVP trophy. I hope I measure up to her expectations.

"I didn't mean to insult the game you love," she says.

"I didn't take it that way." I don't know if I can say the same for Ivan and Tipp. . . .

"I admire your passion for hockey," she says. "To do as well as you've done takes more than just ability. It takes desire and drive. . . . You must want it very badly."

Self-control. Think unsexy thoughts . . . toe jam, jock itch, earwax. . . .

A loud laugh breaks through the thumping background noise. "Subs are here!" someone yells, and a cheer goes up.

"I guess they'll come looking for me," Laura says.

"Do you still want it?"

"Yes. I'm starving, actually."

"Well, let me prepare for the feast."

I pull out the ironing board that Mom keeps in my closet. She sometimes irons in my room because I've got the only upstairs TV. I set it up, spread a blanket over top and add the crowning glory— a candle that I stashed in my night table earlier, just in case.

"Your table, my lady."

*Thump, thump, thump!*

"You lovebirds decent?" It's Ivan outside the door and, from the sound of laughter, about twenty other people, too. I open it. Ivan whistles when he sees the ironing board all set up.

"Check it out, guys!" Most of the guys go "O-o-o-o-o," and the girls go "Aw-w-w-w." Probably later they'll be asking the guys why they don't ever do romantic stuff like that.

Ivan and Tipp lay the sub carefully on the ironing board, like waiters in a fancy restaurant. "Dinner is served," they say. The crowd laughs. Molly's right up front, I notice.

"Thanks for the sub, guys. We can take care of it from here." It's their cue to leave, but they jam up the doorway, laughing.

"I think it's the wrong sub," says Laura. "I just wanted a six-inch."

Loud laughs this time, along with some lewd comments along the lines of "You won't find much that's only six inches long in this room."

"I'll eat half," I say and start to unwrap it. It's heavy and big. A veggie sub shouldn't weigh this much. It's warm, too.

"Wait a minute. Did you guys get the meatball sub or something?"

Snickers. Giggles. Then I unwrap the last bit, and people start screaming. It's not a sub at all. It's a rabbit, dead but still warm. Road kill, I guess, but it's not bloody or anything, just tucked up in the sub paper with its head on its paws as if it's taking a nap. I don't scream, but I guess I jump back because the rabbit falls off the ironing board onto the floor. *Thud.* Now it looks like road kill. I can't help but laugh. What a perfect practical joke. Rabbit food for the lady. Fresh meat for me. I wouldn't have expected such artistry from Ivan and Tipp.

But I should have looked at Laura before I laughed. She's glaring at me like I'm shit on the bottom of her shoe. Without a word she sweeps past me and stands in front of the crowd at the door until they part and let her through. My friends and I stare at each other with the dead rabbit between us. I guess they're waiting for me to do something, and I feel if I hadn't had quite so much to drink, I could think of what to do. It takes the slamming of the front door to snap me out of it.

A few people pat me on the back as I run past them. They say things like, "Geez, it was just a joke." I yank open the front door. Laura's already way down the street, walking straight and tall with her head back, staring up at the moon. Behind me the party starts up again. People are laughing and squealing about the rabbit.

Laura's beautiful, even from the back. I could still catch her if I tried. I could run after her in my sock feet and say what jerks my friends are and what a thoughtless idiot I was for laughing. Part of me wants to run after her. But part of me wants to head back to the party, where it's warm and friendly, where a guy can laugh at a good joke, where there are plenty of girls who would love me without me even trying.

Here's one now. The hands over my eyes are almost as soft as Laura's. They smell like soap. She breathes in my ear, warm breath I could grab with my lips and fall into. . . .

Her hands slide down my face, my chest, my belt. They slip into the front pockets of my jeans.

"Molly . . ." I whisper.

"Shhhh," she whispers back.

And that's the moment Laura turns and sees. She's standing in the halo of the streetlight, looking like she did when she got here, an angel with snowflakes in her hair. I take a quick step forward. Molly's hands slide out of my pockets. Maybe Laura can't see her standing behind me. Maybe . . .

But Laura shakes her head, smiles and walks off into the night. She's on a different course, and it's headed straight away from me.

1993

## bodies

# (Anna)

In the last days of June, a heat wave pressed down on Lee like a big sweaty hand. Sam and I sat on the curb to eat Freezies and watch the construction. Sam was like a kid when it came to that stuff. He knew exactly what the men in hard hats were doing down there in that pit. All I knew was that it had something to do with pipes and water, and it was making a mess of Main Street. Sam explained it to me once, but I was concentrating on the way his new moustache wiggled when he spoke, and I was too embarrassed to ask him again. So I pretended to be bored.

"Let's walk," I said.

Main Street was turning red and white that day. Mr. Papp was painting a big maple leaf on the sub shop window. Mitch's mom was tying balloons outside the Pretty as a Princess Salon. Lil and Babs were stapling plastic flags around the doors at the drugstore.

"I almost forgot about Canada Day," I lied to Sam.

"How could you? It's an annual tradition." He meant the fireworks at the park. We go to see them every year and do something goofy while we're there. Last year we jumped on stage and sang "O Canada" off key at the top of our lungs.

"How can we top last year's performance?" I asked, but I was really wondering if maybe this year we could knock off the kiddie pranks and go like a real boyfriend and girl friend. Find a spot away from the crowd, spread out a blanket and, who knows, maybe make a few fireworks of our own.

It's like we were on the verge of something that could go either way. We could take the plunge into the pit and find out what it's like to get messy, or we could turn and walk away from it. I guess we were both afraid to make the first move and spoil what we'd had for so long.


Sam has been my summer friend since we were six years old. We're neighbors in a way. I live in the last house on the north end of town, and Sam lives on the first farm. Between his fields and my backyard is a cedar bush with a stream running through it. You never know what will come floating down that stream from the center of town. Ducks, sometimes, and empty pop bottles that, as kids, we fished out and filled with messages: *Shipwrecked! Help!* And we signed them with our code names for each other: Sam-I-am and Annabanana.

Near the edge of the stream is a tank-sized boulder we used to pretend was a pirate ship. There's a tall spindly maple tree growing right up beside it that we used for a mast, but the best part is the secret hiding place underneath the boulder—a tiny cave just big enough for two kids to sit in cross-legged, side by side. We called it the brig. The entrance was almost completely hidden by ferns, and we hid in there more than once when we were being chased by Vikings or aliens or whoever we dreamed up to be our enemies. It had been years since we played like that, but we still used the "deck" on top of the boulder for picnics.

Come September, Sam and I go our separate ways, each with our own set of school friends. But every June, Sam shows up at my back door and asks for Annabanana, or I show up at his and ask for Sam-I-am, and we have a great time all summer long. Or we used to. This summer it all felt different. Not bad different, just not as comfortable as it used to be. For one thing Sam finally got taller than me and bigger, too, as if he'd been working out with weights or something. I kept misjudging where my body ended and his began, and sometimes, when we walked side by side, the backs of our hands would touch, and we'd both jerk back, as if we felt an electric shock or something.

We stopped at the bulletin board outside the bank to see if anyone had taken my phone number from my baby-sitting poster. Two of the little flaps of paper with my number written on them were gone.

"I don't like your number plastered all over the board," said Sam. "Anyone could take it. Like this sicko."

He pointed to a new poster that was rammed up beside mine. It read: ERECTION SPECIALIST! (Gazebos and sheds.) No job too small!

"I can take care of myself, Sam."

"Yeah? Well, did you hear the news this morning? Another girl is missing."

I hadn't heard. Maybe that explained the strange hushed feeling on Main Street that day. It's probably what the smoky circle of grey-haired ladies was gossiping about in Donut Heaven, and what Lil and Babs were clucking their tongues about as they stapled up flags around the drugstore doors.

Another girl. That made three girls in three months. Some psycho copycat killer was doing what they say Paul Bernardo did to those poor girls last year and the year before. It was the nightmare all over again, except this time it was even scarier because it was closer to home. The psycho killer guy (that's how I thought of him—Psycho Killer Guy) abducted girls from Toronto, but dumped their bodies here, around Lee. They found the first one, Lynda Gavin, in a ditch on the sixth concession, and the second one, Sarah Hamilton, in a field where they've started construction on a new subdivision. Sam told me the third girl's name was Marissa White.

"Sam?" I said. "Do you think the killer is one of us?" What I meant was could he be from Lee?

"Could be," said Sam. "Maybe it's that guy parked outside the Meat Shop."

"Yeah," I whispered, "or that guy sitting outside the Co-op."

Sam made his eyes go shifty. "Or it could be me."

I swatted his arm. Electric shock number three for the day. "Don't even joke about it! Maybe it's not a *guy* at all."

"Oh please." Sam pretended to throw up in the garbage can as we passed it.

"Anyway, I'm sure he's a stranger," I said. "He's probably got a cottage up north and dumps the bodies on his way through town."

The bodies. We talked about them like they were garbage. I couldn't put the two things together, those pretty smiling faces on TV and the bodies. On the news, they show you the black body bag strapped onto a stretcher, as if it's all right to show that, as if there's not some poor dead girl inside. I tried to imagine what they looked like, the bodies. I'd never seen one, not even in a funeral parlor.

I knew what those girls looked like before, when they were girls and not just bodies. Their school photos were plastered all over the TV and newspapers. The creepy thing was they looked a bit like me. They both had green eyes and braces on their teeth and brown curly hair. I read that Lynda had wanted to become an acupuncturist someday, and Sarah had wanted to be a chef. The police said the girls died of multiple stab wounds. My theory was that maybe Psycho Killer Guy had a thing about knives and sharp objects, and wanted to save the girls from becoming a psychopathic stabbing monster like himself.

Sam told me that Marissa White was abducted from her part-time job at a hair salon. Scissors, I thought! Razors!

I was telling Sam my theory when we walked past Vera, who was sitting, as usual, on the bench outside the A & P. We called her Vera because we didn't know her real name. She appeared out of nowhere in the spring, wearing about twenty layers of clothes and dragging a bundle buggy behind her. It looked like she'd peeled off most of the layers and packed them into the bundle buggy. Sam said she was like an old snake hoarding its skins.

That day, Vera was wearing striped Bermuda shorts with a grimy pink tank top, foam sandals and a floppy straw hat. Her legs were covered with spider veins and coarse black hairs, and she needed a bath. I could smell her BO from the corner. But what I noticed most was her bony arms and legs. I hadn't realized before how awfully thin she was under all those layers of clothes.

"She's sympt-o-matic," Sam's dad said. "All part of the Toronna crap that's moving north with the commuters. First they build subdivisions and then low income housing, and then you'll see what'll happen. That woman's just the beginning."

Vera never asked for money. I almost wished she would. I'd always wanted to talk to her but would chicken out when I got close.

"Sam," I whispered when I thought we were out of earshot, "do you think Vera will still be here come winter?"

Sam shrugged. "I heard some church folks got her a place, but she wouldn't go."

"You mean she *wants* to live outside?"

"I guess so. Maybe she was a hippie or something."

"Sam, look!" Lying at my feet was a crisp twenty-dollar bill. The top end of the street was deserted. Whoever had dropped it was long gone.

Sam picked it up and whistled. "Nice one. Brand new. I guess this means you're buying lunch today."

"Nope! I know just what to do with it."

Sam just shook his head when I told him and gave me one of those looks that I'd never seen before this summer.

"Sweet Annabanana," he said.

The first part of my plan went off without a hitch. We turned around and walked past Vera, talking about the weather, not even looking at her. Then I pulled my hand out of my pocket and, as if by accident, dropped the twenty at her feet. We walked as fast as we could to the corner, but the light turned red and we had to stop.

"Miss! Hey, Miss!" Vera's voice was dry and gritty as if her throat was full of sand. "You dropped this." She shoved the twenty into my hand. I think her eyes under the floppy brim were laughing at me. She turned and stomped back to her bench.

Sam was stifling giggles. "She doesn't want your handouts," he whispered, "but I'm not proud. How about subs for lunch?" I hauled off and gave him a good swat. Electric shock number four for the day.

After lunch we cooled off in the above-ground pool that Mom complained was a terrible eyesore. She sometimes threatened to tear it down and put in a proper vegetable garden. But Sam said the pool was the reason he came around so much, and if she got rid of it, he'd have to go, too. Then he'd present her with the basket of tomatoes or beans or peppers that he'd brought from home, and we wouldn't hear another word of complaint from Mom. She adored Sam. She said if she'd ever had a son, she'd want him to be just like Sam.

He didn't wear one of those little Spandex bathing suits, thank goodness. I wouldn't have known where to look if he did. Instead he'd cut the legs off some old jeans and wore those. I'd seen those jeans many times over the winter, but I had no idea what was happening underneath them. Hair had grown all over Sam's body—curly blond hair that looked springy to the touch.

"You should start shaving, Sam," I teased on the way out to the pool. His hand went up to his little moustache. He thought I meant his face.

Mom waved from where she was weeding the flower bed.

"Tomatoes are in the kitchen!" called Sam.

Mom laughed and yelled, "Thanks." She watched us climb onto the pool deck. Watched Sam, I should say. She raised her eyebrows at me and winked. I could have died. But I don't think Sam saw. He was pulling off his T-shirt. Up past his stomach and chest it went, revealing hair that curled around his nipples like fine copper wire. Nipples! I never thought of Sam as having nipples before or any other body part for that matter. Suddenly I realized that the only thing between me and the rest of Sam was a thin layer of woven denim fibres. I figured we'd better get swimming—fast.

Sam beat me to it. He took a two-step run for it, turned himself into a cannonball and doused me with a million freezing drops of water.

"You're gonna get it now!" I hurled myself after him. We had a water war, pulling legs, grabbing waists, tackling each other. *Zap! Zap! Zap!* One shock after another. They say you're supposed to keep electricity away from water, but I don't think they meant the kind that was charging the pool that day. It wasn't the kind that kills. It was the kind that brings you to life.

We stopped to catch our breath. Sam's face was so close to mine, I could see the beads of water clinging to the hairs of his moustache. That crazy moustache. I still hadn't decided if I liked it or not, that strange thing on the face I knew so well. But I wanted to know it better, know what it felt like pressed against my own upper lip.

I could see my reflection in Sam's blue eyes, distorted, as if I were looking into a fun house mirror. I guess Sam could see his reflection in my eyes, too. It made me think of those pictures within pictures within pictures that go on forever, and I wondered if that's how it was with Sam and me.

Sam swallowed hard as if he had something huge to say and couldn't get it out. Under water, our fingertips met and reached into one another as far as they could go. We pressed our palms together and squeezed so hard it almost hurt. My hand had been in Sam's a thousand times before, when we were little and played clapping games and thumb wrestled. But this was completely different. I'm not sure why we held on so tight. I think that huge thing Sam wanted to say was coming through his fingers instead of his lips.

Finally he let go. His fingers, which had felt so strong and fierce, turned gentle and started tracing circles over the backs of my hands and the palms and around and around my fingernails, and if the water hadn't been so cold, I think I would have melted.

Then it was my turn. I touched the rough nubs of his knuckles and the smooth webbed place between his fingers at the base. His eyes fluttered closed when I touched him there.

He let out his breath. I did, too. I didn't realize that I'd been holding it. I giggled, and finally Sam broke a smile.

Above the water nothing much had changed, but below the surface everything was different. We sank lower—chins, lips, noses, eyes—until we were all the way under, all the way different. Now every part of Sam looked blue and dappled with shadows from the poplar trees that rustled around the pool. Leaf shadows raced up and down my own blue arms, and I wondered if I looked as different to Sam as he did to me. Then the only blue I saw was Sam's eyes, enormous and questioning, as our lips met, backed away, then met again. Just like our fingers, they touched for longer each time, pressing into each other, slowly and gently like slippers and silky feet trying each other on.

I don't know how long we were down there before my lungs started finger tapping, then pounding, on my brain: *Time to breathe!* When we burst upward, gasping and laughing, the trees were still rustling, Mom was still gardening. Amazingly, unbelievably, everything in the world above the water was the same. We clung below the edge of the pool so Mom couldn't see us. I knew I had a big silly grin all over my face just like the one on Sam's.

"Sam-I-am," I whispered. "I like your moustache."

I took down my baby-sitting poster and got some names instead from my own old baby-sitter, Jewel. I got three regular baby-sitting jobs that way, evenings and weekends mostly, but usually Sam would come over so it wasn't too bad.

It was safer with two we decided. And to protect each other even more, after we tucked the kids into bed, we'd snuggle close on the couch. With one ear listening for the kids and the other ear listening for the parents coming home, I'd let the rest of me get lost in his Sam-ness.

He had the most amazing smell, like fresh air and hay and soap all rolled into one. He said he didn't know what it was. "Mom uses Tide and hangs the clothes on the line. Maybe that's it," he said. But it was more than just his clothes. It was his skin, tanned and rough in spots, pale and soft in others. Feeling like a happy tipsy traveler lost in a strange and wonderful city, I'd turn the corner behind his ear or his knee and discover tender spots I never knew were there.

"I could eat you up, you taste so good," Sam said, nibbling the back of my neck. We'd discovered that if I could keep the tickles under control when he kissed me there, it felt phenomenal. Way better than fireworks. More like a nuclear explosion.

"If warm had a taste," said Sam, "it would be you." What a guy.

One night, we were baby-sitting Jewel's own three kids, and after we put them to bed, we watched the movie *Psycho* on TV. Sam was afraid I'd find it too scary, but I wanted to see it. Everyone's seen *Psycho*.

I spread my fingers like a fan over my eyes, but I saw everything. I saw the woman in the shower and the shadow of the knife through the shower curtain before it plunged—*Eee! Eee! Eee!*—in time to the music.

That got me thinking about Lynda and Sarah. I wondered if Psycho Killer Guy had dressed up like a woman or someone else. I wondered if that's why they went with him in the first place—because he didn't look like a Psycho Killer Guy. Like Paul Bernardo, for instance, the guy they arrested not long ago. What's so scary about him? He's got a nice face, a nice smile. He could be any of the guys in my school. He could be Sam, for that matter. Yet they say he killed those two girls, Leslie Mahaffey and Kristen French.

And since I was thinking about Paul Bernardo and being dressed up, I remembered the wedding picture they showed on the news of Bernardo and his wife Karla, in a horse drawn carriage. They had a big splashy wedding like the mock royal wedding they put on at the high school ten years ago, when I was picked to be a flower girl for the pretend Prince Charles and Lady Diana. Sam says that's why I'm a romantic: I was engineered to be one from the time I was five years old and took part in a fairy-tale wedding. That's what Bernardo's was—a fairy-tale wedding. Except, on the very same day he married his princess, Leslie Mahaffey's body was found cut into pieces and packed in cement. Some prince.

I wondered if Psycho Killer Guy had seen the movie *Psycho*. I wondered if he set those girls up in a nice warm shower, and just when they were relaxed and happy, he stabbed them through the shower curtain while music screeched in the background: *Eee! Eee! Eee! DIE! DIE! DIE!*

"I knew we shouldn't have watched it," said Sam. "Try not to let it bug you."

But it did bug me. It bugged me so much that I signed up for the field searches around town. They were still looking for Marissa White. I hoped we wouldn't find her. To find her would mean she was dead. I kept hoping that this girl would outwit Psycho Killer Guy and live. I hoped they'd find the girl and not just a body.

Two weeks after Canada Day, the heat wave broke with a thunderstorm so mighty, it was like the fireworks all over again, except this time it was real, white, deadly lightning slicing through the sky. I had a bit of a phobia about lightning left over from when I was a kid. I went to bed early and covered my ears with a pillow and tried to block out the storm by thinking about Sam. We had planned to spend the next day together, a whole glorious day.

Luckily by morning, the storm had passed and taken with it the awful heat. It was a beautiful day. A perfect day. I met Sam in the cedar bush, and we walked along the trail remembering the stuff we used to do as kids. We poked around the remains of the tree fort we tried to build one year, and the pile of rocks where we'd buried a dead blue jay. Sam had brought some lemonade in a thermos and some oatmeal cookies his mom made. He carried them in a knapsack in his left hand and put his right arm around my shoulders. When the path grew too narrow, we turned sideways and walked like crabs. Sometimes Sam kissed my neck while we walked. He stubbed his toe on a tree root that way.

As we headed for our pirate-ship boulder, we heard the singsong voice of a kid. We looked at each other, disappointed. Finding a place to be alone was almost impossible when neither one of us was driving yet. A chubby little girl was standing on the boulder, curtseying toward the stream. I didn't recognize her. She was wearing a scruffy pink dress with matching mosquito bites up and down her legs. She was chattering away in the kind of little kid chipmunk voice that I can never understand. It reminded me of the few times Sam agreed to play prince and princess with me, except, I guess, this little girl's prince was imaginary.

As we watched, Sam's fingers started playing air guitar on my ribs.

"Quit it! That tickles!" I laughed. The little girl spun around, almost losing her balance.

"Careful!" I called to her. "I fell off there once and that *doesn't* tickle!"

She got down on all fours and shimmied down the far side of the boulder.

"Hey, do your parents know where you are?" called Sam, but she was already running off into the trees.

"You scared her, Sam."

"She shouldn't be out here by herself. It's not safe."

"You want to be everyone's bodyguard."

He kissed me. "Mostly yours."

We munched our cookies in the usual way, lying on our stomachs on top of the boulder, watching the stream below. It was swollen and running fast from the rain the night before. We laughed at a pair of ducks that bobbed past enjoying the ride.

Then I saw it. My cookie fell and landed right beside it. That's when Sam saw it, too. Not three feet away from the bank of the stream was a hand covered in grime, barely visible through the ferns at the base of the boulder.

"Jesus," croaked Sam.

"Is it . . . real?" I whispered. Of course it was real. Who would put a fake hand out here in the woods? But I couldn't believe it.

Sam was looking around us. Suddenly I wasn't seeing trees. I was seeing hundreds of hiding places.

"Do you think he's still here?" I whispered.

"I doubt it," Sam whispered back. "Not in broad daylight."

"Oh my God, Sam! That little girl was right here! Do you think she saw it?"

He shook his head. He was sitting up now, staring at the

hand. All of a sudden I wanted to hurry. Maybe she—Marissa—by some miracle was still alive.

"Come on, Sam! We have to go see!"

"I'll go," said Sam. "You stay here."

"No way, I'm coming, too." I wanted to look. I didn't want to look. But either way I wanted to stay close to Sam.

I held my breath as we jumped off the boulder and tiptoed to the ferns. Sam was in front of me, a patch of sweat the size of Lake Simcoe spreading down the back of his T-shirt.

"Sam, wait." He turned. He looked different, scared, like a little boy. I took his hand. "On the count of three, okay?" I said.

He nodded. We counted to three.

I had imagined this moment many times. Finding Marissa. I imagined her clean and tragically beautiful, dressed in white maybe and laid out like Snow White, sleeping a deathlike sleep. But I knew that whatever lay at the other end of that grimy hand probably wasn't clean and beautiful. I prayed that at least her eyes would be shut. I never liked it in the movies when the bodies' eyes were open and staring.

"One . . . two . . . three."

With our free hands we parted the ferns. Whatever else I had been expecting, it wasn't this. The woman who was curled up dead in our hiding place wasn't Marissa White. It was Vera. She was wearing the same pink tank top and striped Bermuda shorts, but now they were caked with mud. So was her hair. It was so matted that I could hardly see her face, but I knew she was dead. Her staring eyes were no longer filled with disdain or anything else. They were empty and lifeless as two glass marbles.

That was all I saw before Sam stumbled back and made me lose my balance on the slippery bank. I almost recovered, but a whole chunk of soggy grass gave way. Still holding hands, we splashed backward into the stream. The water was muddy and strong. I struggled to stand, but slipped again, this time cracking my head on a rock.

"Ow!" I swallowed a mouthful of awful-tasting water.

Sam grabbed me by the arm and yanked.

"*Ow!*" I yelled.

"I'm sorry. I'm sorry!" cried Sam.

We climbed out where a flat rock gave more solid footing, about twenty feet downstream from the boulder. Sam made me lie down. Gently he wiped a piece of grass off my cheek and cupped his hand behind my neck. I thought he was either going to start artificial respiration or kiss me, but he didn't do either. He just looked at me, scared, but not like a little boy anymore. His jaw was clenched and worry lines wrinkled his forehead. *This is what Sam will look like when he's an old man,* I thought.

"Sam . . . I'm all right. I just hit my head, that's all."

"Let me see. . . . Shit, you're bleeding! I'll carry you home."

"I can walk, Sam, really."

We decided to leave Vera where she was and get help. We rushed back along the trail, Sam's arm tight around my shoulders. He seemed more concerned about knocking me into the stream than he was about Vera, but I couldn't get my mind off her. So thin, skin over bones, curled into a ball to comfort herself.

"Sam? Have you ever seen a . . . you know . . . a body before?"

"Not like that. Just at funerals, when they're all cleaned up."

His voice sounded different, deeper. I think he was trying not to gag. He was quiet until we got home and told Mom what had happened.

"I didn't mean to hurt her," Sam said. The look on his face reminded me of our eight-year-old neighbor who pitched a baseball through our bay window last year. He came to the door so upset he could hardly speak. Sam was looking at Mom the same way now, as if I was a precious window he'd broken.

Mom called the police and dabbed the cut on my head with

disinfectant while we waited for them to arrive. Sam said he had to use the washroom, but instead of heading for the downstairs powder room, he went upstairs. Ten minutes later, he was still there.

"Sam?" I yelled up the stairs. "Sam!" I ran up two at a time.

Through the bathroom door, I could hear him throwing up. It was awful—violent retching, coughing, spitting—and then . . . a sob.

"Sam? . . . You okay?"

Running water. The toilet flushing. "Yeah. Fine." His voice was deep. He was old-man Sam again.

"You coming down now?"

"I'll be a minute."

I got the feeling that he didn't want me to wait for him.

"I'll see you downstairs then. . . ."

"Yeah, see ya."

*See ya?* That's what we said at the end of our dates and phone calls. Is it what you say after finding a dead body, too? I'd never wondered what to say to Sam before. Now I did.


Dr. Meyers is the coroner as well as our family doctor, so after he examined me, he must have examined Vera. It kind of freaked me out when I realized later that his hands were on both of us in the same day. Living, dead—it's a small but major difference, a heart-beat, that's all.

The local paper said that Vera's real name was Betty Mace and she used to live here in Lee on my very street until her family moved away when she was six. I figured she must have known about that hiding place under the boulder and gone there for shelter from the rain, gone there to die. She was full of cancer, the article said, and swallowed some pills that she got from a doctor in the city. An overdose. That made sense to me. I couldn't imag-

101

ine Vera—Betty, I mean—hooked up to tubes in a hospital, dying slowly, inch by inch.

Instead I imagined her as a chubby little girl in a scruffy pink dress with mosquito bites and a head full of dreams, squatting in the brig beneath a pirate-ship boulder, watching the world from behind a screen of fresh green ferns.

I called Sam to tell him. We'd hardly seen each other in the past few days. Sam said he was extra busy on the farm and too tired to come over in the evenings.

"Annabanana . . . such a romantic," he sighed. But I knew who the real romantic was. Sam was the one who had wanted to carry me home and be my knight in shining armor.

"Anna, they found Marissa White's body today."

"Oh God. Where?"

"In the old silo on Bells' farm."

I wanted it all to go away. The death, the bodies, the nightmares about knives. Always the knives. Even in my dreams of Sam.

Just the night before, I dreamed we were in his room in the farmhouse, and it smelled like Sam, like fresh air and hay and soap, and he was telling me he loved me—God, how he loved me—and the electric shocks were coming so fast, I felt electrocuted with happiness. I thought nothing could ever scare me again, not as long as I was with Sam.

Then in the dream our clothes were off, and it felt so right. Sam said once, *Are you sure?* And I said, *Yes. Yes!*

Then I felt it.

Like a knife slicing through my middle, even though this knife was screaming: *Live! Live! LIVE!* I didn't know it would hurt so bad. I didn't know Sam would hurt me.

It was just a dream, but not just a dream. The same way *Psycho* wasn't just a movie. I felt different talking to Sam now, as if we'd crossed a line and couldn't go back. And, oh, I wanted to go back!

Back to that blue shadowy moment in the swimming pool with just our hands pressed together in the promise of things to come.

"I miss you, Sam," I whispered into the phone.

His voice sounded far away, and I couldn't tell if he was my Sam or little-boy Sam or old-man Sam.

"I miss you, too," he said.

# (Mitch)

*Br-r-r-ring! Br-r-r-ring!*

So much for sweet dreams. I hate people who call early. Mom starts banging on my door. She *knows* I never take calls before nine.

"Mitch? It sounds important. Someone from the nursing home."

The nursing home! That gets me up. For one awful second, I'm sure Rosetta has gone and done something terrible like died. But it's Rosetta on the phone.

"Today is the day, my dear!"

"The day for what?"

"The twins, Michelle! They come today!"

"Get outta town!"

"I will *not* 'get outta town,' not when my girls are finally coming." Rosetta's worse than an English teacher, correcting what I say. I don't mind, though. It rolls off me now.

"Wow! I can't wait to meet them." It's true. I can't believe they're actually here, actually *real*. I've been listening to Rosetta brag about her twin girls for weeks now. How they're so beautiful and smart, how they vacation with royalty and dine with princes, lah-dee-dah, and aren't they special? Who wouldn't think that was a load of crap? But I guess now that they're here, I'll be able to see for myself.

"I hope you *will* see them, Michelle. What time are you coming?"

"The usual, I guess. Ten? What time'll the girls be there?"

"I think they'll be here soon, but I'm not certain of the time. Oh dear. . . ." She starts sounding worried. That's all she needs— a heart attack on the day her daughters finally decide to show their faces.

"Well don't get your knickers in a twist!" Rosetta always says that to me. Now I can finally throw it back at her. "If they come sooner than ten, call me. If it's later, I'll be there anyway. Have no fear, there's *no way* I'm gonna miss meeting *these* girls."

Rosetta Teodosovich is ninety-three years old. She lives in the only private room in the Buckingham Suites Nursing Home, where everyone acts like she's the queen. She acts like it, too. Takes it for granted the housekeepers will clean up her messes, the nurses will wash and dress her, and if they don't do it right, hoo haw, look out!

It's all a scam. Really she's a softie, but no one's guessed it but me. Rosetta said she "let me in" because I'm "cut from the same cloth." I guess what she means is I'm a scammer, too.

We laugh about how my visiting her is supposed to be a punishment, my community service. 'Course when we laugh, it's gotta be with the door closed. Can't let Miss Knabb, director of nursing, hear us having a good time. Knabb hates me. Hates me with a passion. Her aunt, Mrs. Wiggen, is one of the ol' biddies I scammed.

This was the scam.

Stashed way in the back of the student council closet at school, I found a box of souvenir programs from the royal wedding. Not the real wedding, but the mock wedding the high school put on in '82, a year after Prince Charles and Lady Diana got married. My day care teacher, Jewel, had the part of Diana, and she got me a part, too. I was a flower girl, the cute little blonde one. All dressed up, with a dye job courtesy of Ma's salon, I was a dead ringer for the real flower girl, maybe even a shade cuter!

Everyone said I stole the show. There were even close-ups of me on cable TV! When people asked us to sign their programs, I drew little happy faces with crowns on them since I couldn't write yet. They were glitzy programs, full color, same as the ones I found in the box. The price on the cover said ten bucks. I figured they'd be worth even more now, especially with the real royal marriage on the rocks.

So I smuggled out the box and started selling them door to door in the seniors apartment building for the bargain price of fifteen dollars. Collector's items, I told them! A real steal! I threw in my signature, with my trademark crown 'n' happy face, for free. The best part, I told them, was the profits would go to the Buckingham Suites Nursing Home. Great scam, eh?

Trouble was, by the time I trudged up and down those hallways, my shoes wore out and I had to buy new ones and some new clothes to go with them, and, well, by the time I was done shopping, there weren't any profits left for the Buckingham Suites. Oh well, I figured, what they don't know won't hurt them. Turns out, what they didn't know, hurt me! Mrs. Wiggen in 3A got suspicious and called her niece, Miss Knabb, at the nursing home, and the rest is history. I got nailed. Knabbed.

Go directly to community service! Do not pass GO! Do not collect $200! Just the opposite. Mom had to pay back the people I scammed, and now I'm stuck working at Ma's hair salon to pay off what I owe her.

But the part I was really dreading was having to do time at the nursing home. That was Knabb's idea. She got right involved in my "rehabilitation and education," as she calls it. She demanded to be at the meeting in my vice principal's office. The usual crew was there—me, Ma, the guidance counselor and the vice. This time Janet somebody from the police department was there, too, and so was Miss Knabb, looking stiff and sour as a dill pickle. The usual crew said they weren't sure what to do with me. They'd told me before: I had to Tell the Truth, Take Responsibility for my Actions, Think Before I Act, blah, blah, blah . . .

Knabb started rolling her eyes and said I was headed for real trouble if I wasn't straightened out now. Credit card fraud! Telemarketing scams! Maybe even armed robbery! Okay so she didn't exactly say all those things but she *looked* them at me. And then she suggested I do my community service at the nursing home so I'd get to know the kind of people I'd hurt.

Buckingham Suites is no palace, that's for sure. You have to punch in a code to get in and out, or you set off the alarm. And they said I wouldn't be in jail! The stench of pee hit me as soon as I walked in. I figured Knabb would have me washing diapers and scrubbing bedpans, but she said she had something different in mind for me. My community service was to visit (and, I figured, be a personal slave to) two "residents with attitude": Hank Phipps, keeper of the courtyard garden, and Rosetta Teodosovich, queen of the nursing home.

Dead easy, right? But I kept getting lost in that maze of hallways, and every time I asked for directions to Rosetta's room, people would look at me like I was crazy.

"Going to see the Dragon Lady?" one guy in a bathrobe muttered. "Good luck to ye, m'dear."

When I finally found the door that said *R. Teodosovich, Knock before Entering,* a Mack truck of a housekeeper came flying out and almost bowled me over.

"I wouldn't go in there," she said, patting down her steel-wool hair. "She's in one ripsnorter of a mood."

Enough is enough, I figured. How scary could one old lady be?

"Mrs. T?" I started to push open the door.

"KNNNOCK!" The voice inside bellowed.

So I knocked a peppy tune: Knock, knock, knock-knock, knock—KNOCK, KNOCK!

"Enter," said the voice. It was hard to believe such a big voice came from such a little lady. She was propped up in bed, wearing a fancy, pink satin nightie. She wore red lipstick and bright blue eye shadow, but it was her hair that was amazing. There was more of it than there was of her. Braided into a thick grey rope, it slithered over her shoulder, down her caved-in chest and disappeared under the bedspread. Her fingers were twisted and lumpy. She kept sticking them in and out of a fluffy ball of wool in her lap.

"Call me 'Mrs. T' one more time," she said, "and I will throw a book at you." The books stacked on her night table looked thick and deadly, and she had about two hundred more filling the floor-to-ceiling shelves.

"I didn't want to say your name wrong."

"Say it."

"Mrs. Uh—Tee-oh-dah-saw-vitch?"

"You did say it incorrectly. You may call me Rosetta. And you are Michelle Tyne?"

"I go by Mitch."

"'Mitch' is a wretched name for a girl. I shall call you Michelle. Now, Michelle, I am told that you are a criminal. Tell me. . . ." Her eyes were bullets boring into me. "Can you break me out of here?"

"Are you kidding? I doubt I'll find my own way back outta here!"

She grunted.

"Come here, Michelle. Closer." She squinted her bullet eyes at me.

"You are a nasty girl," she said finally. "You have nasty eyes."

Great, I thought, here two minutes and already she hates me. Knabb'll say it's just what she expected.

"Ho, ho! Michelle, you misunderstand. By 'nasty eyes,' I mean they will break the hearts of men. Unless they have already, hmm?" Her bullet eyes twinkled at me. She was joking, the scammer!

"Well, Rosetta, I guess that's for me to know and for you to find out."

She laughed again. "Very good, Michelle. A woman without secrets is a dull person indeed. Now, do you see these books?" As if I could miss them. I never saw so many books in one little room before.

"I would like you to read them to me," said Rosetta.

Oh man! So that's my real punishment, I figured. It was going to be worse than jail. It was going to be a frigging English class!

"You *do* read?" said Rosetta.

"Sure, I can read. But don't ask me to slog through those things!" Even if I could stay awake to do it, I wasn't about to break my record of never reading a book cover to cover. I worked long and hard to build up my network of browner friends and collection of Coles notes, and I wasn't about to change for ol' Rosetta Teodosovich.

"No, no," she said. "Not whole books. We haven't time. Just my favorite bits."

"I guess I can read 'bits.'"

"Hair is the other thing," she said. "I despise this braid, but it's all the nurses will do, and I don't trust the visiting hairdresser. She gossips. Can you style hair?"

"Can I?! My ma's a hairdresser, for Pete's sake! I've been styling hair since I was three years old. Had a whole bunch of heads to play with."

"Heads?"

"Yeah, you know those fake heads with hair? I had every

color—blonde, brunette, red. I remember asking Ma where she stashed the bodies."

"Ho, ho! A regular Bluebeard's castle!"

"I guess. Anyway, Rosetta, what it means is I can style your hair just about any way you like."

"Can you manage a French roll?"

"I can do a French roll blindfolded."

"Try it with your eyes open, Michelle, and we have a deal."

I figured I wouldn't mind doing something with that long snaky hair. And it wouldn't kill me to read the odd "bit" from a book. I decided I was going to like Rosetta. She sure wasn't like any ol' lady I ever met. She wasn't like anyone else, period.


For once, I'm not late. Five to ten, I'm outside Rosetta's door, ready to knock. I can already hear a party going on inside. Loud excited voices jabber away in the language Rosetta uses when she swears at the nurses, except this time the voices are happy. I figure the girls probably just got here and don't need me crashing the reunion in the first few minutes. I decide to go visit Hank first and come back when things have calmed down.

I can't resist peeking in, though. I just see bits and pieces through the crack in the door, but it's them all right. Gotta be! I'm seeing three Rosettas, except two of them are a lot younger. It's the twins all right. Erika and Stella. They're dressed way too fancy for visiting a nursing home and too young for their age. They look kind of silly, if you ask me, decked out in ruffles and lace and rosebuds in their hair, but maybe they dressed that way to please Rosetta.

One lady is brushing Rosetta's hair the way she likes it, not too gentle at the roots, while the other lady paints Rosetta's nails with the Savage Red nail polish I brought in one day. Rosetta likes to wear it on her ornery days, as she calls them. She looks anything but ornery today, though. She's beaming like the sun itself.

I find Hank in the courtyard, deadheading the flowers.

"That's what you calls it," Hank says, "when you lops off the old blooms so the new ones can grow."

"Then OFF WITH THEIR HEADS!" I say.

Hank says I'd make a great queen; I'm just a late bloomer.

"Buckingham Suites already has a queen," I tell him, but Hank says, "Naw, Rosetta's just an ol' deadhead."

Hank and Rosetta don't get along. I tried once to get them together. I got Rosetta spiffed up with Savage Red nail polish and matching lipstick, and rolled her out here in a wheelchair to meet Hank. I figured they'd hit it off or at least get into a good cock fight.

Well, sparks *did* fly, just not the right kind. Hank told a joke about a lonely broke ol' lady whose only companion is a mangy cat. One day, while she's collecting bottles, a genie pops outta one and says the lady can have three wishes. So she wishes to be young and beautiful and—poof—she is! A real knockout. Red lipstick and everything. Then she wishes for a palace to live in and—poof! There's a castle so huge and fancy, it makes Buckingham Palace look like a doghouse. Then she wishes for her cat, which she loves more than anything, to be turned into a prince, and—poof! He turns into a gorgeous, mouth-watering hunk of a prince!

So the lady's thinking life is pretty near perfect, but then she sees the prince crying. "What's the matter, darling?" she asks.

The prince looks at her sad as anything and says "Dear lady, *now* aren't you sorry you had me fixed?"

Hank told it better. He told a few more jokes, rude ones. Maybe he was nervous and didn't know what else to say. Rosetta knew what to say, though.

"Take me away from this nasty man."

"But nasty's good, right, Rosetta? You said so the first day I met you. Remember? You said I had 'nasty eyes'?"

"Words have many meanings, my dear, and in this case, your Mr. Phipps is just plain nasty."

I think it's Hank's name Rosetta objects to. She hoped it was short for something, but Hank said, "No, it's just Hank, as in *hankie.*"

Rosetta's husband had quite the handle: Ludwig Alfred Teodosovich. Rosetta says he was named after King Ludwig II of Bavaria, the guy who built the fairy-tale castle with all the spires and turrets, the one Disney uses for its logo. Rosetta said when her husband died, she had a stone carving of that same castle put on her husband's gravestone.

Then I guess since we were talking about names and stones and stuff, she told me why her parents called her Rosetta.

Her dad was an archaeologist, and Rosetta was born when he was working in Egypt. He named her after the Rosetta Stone, which Rosetta said was real important. Something was written on it in three different languages—Egyptian hieroglyphs, Greek and I forget what else.

"Do you *see,* Michelle?" Rosetta asked me. "Do you *see* how important the stone was? It was the key to understanding the hieroglyphs. Before the stone was found, hieroglyphs were merely pictures without meaning. But after, translation was possible. Their meaning became clear. Scholars could finally understand the ancient texts—not just what was written on the Rosetta Stone, but countless others as well. It was as if they had been illiterate for years and could suddenly read!"

I'm used to Rosetta's speeches. Sometimes I tune her out, but sometimes what she says makes sense. When she told me about the Rosetta Stone, I knew just what she meant about hard words and pictures without meaning.

"Right on, Rosetta! You got the right name. You're my Rosetta Stone."

It's true. Before I knew Rosetta, trying to slog through books for school was like those poor guys in Egypt trying to figure out the hieroglyphs. The only picture that used to pop into my head while I was reading was one of me throwing the book against a wall.

But Rosetta changed that. She'd talk about what we were reading. "Setting the scene," she called it. She made the words mean something, I guess, so they put pictures in my head. Some of the head pictures, as she called them, were actually kind of interesting, and every so often—just once in a while, mind you—I read a sentence that I wouldn't mind reading again.

The head picture business started with that book, *A Tale of Two Cities.*

"We did this one in school," I told Rosetta when I saw it on her shelf. "What a snoozerama."

"Dickens made you sleepy?"

"Rosetta, it's *boring!*"

"If you found Dickens boring, then perhaps you had the wrong teacher."

Me and my big mouth. Rosetta decided we had to read that one next. But before I even opened the cover, Rosetta made me close my eyes. She talked about what Paris was like back then, before the French Revolution, when people were buried alive in prisons and starving in the streets, when rich noblemen rushed around in fancy coaches running over babies, stopping just long enough to toss a few coins to the poor wailing parents.

After she got me half-interested in the story, she made me read her favorite bits—like when the wine cart spilled and red wine ran like blood through the streets and the starving people got red-stained faces from licking it off the ground. And the parts with crazy ol' Madame Defarge from the wine shop, who knit all the time—a long shapeless thing that looked like nothing. But what it really was, was a list of names in code of the enemies of the revolution who were gonna get their heads chopped on the guillotine.

I saw those heads clear as day, looking just like the ones I used to play with. ONE! There went the blonde with ringlets. TWO! There went the brunette with the bad perm. THREE! There went the redhead with freckles—

"Bravo!" said Rosetta. "You see? The words created pictures in your head, you molded them according to your own experience and suddenly the story came to life!"

We even read the ending of that book 'cause Rosetta loves it so much. She made me close my eyes again and set it up for me, filling in the parts of the story that I'd missed. I hate to admit it, but by the time I finished reading the last page to her, we both had tears in our eyes.

Rosetta's the only person I know who says it's okay to read the ending first. "The pleasure of books," she says, "is that you can close the cover before the last few pages and imagine the ending any way you like."

I think Rosetta makes up her own endings, 'cause sometimes when I'm reading, she'll get this dreamy look and start pulling like crazy at the ball of wool in her lap. She says it helps her fingers. But I think if her hands weren't so crippled with arthritis, Rosetta would be knitting like Madame Defarge. Knitting a stone with different languages or a story with different endings.

"You seem far away today," says Hank. "What's on your mind?"

"Rosetta's twin girls are finally here," I tell him, "and I'm dying to meet them. They're practically superstars!"

I tell Hank what I know—that they live in England where Erika decorates homes of the rich and famous, and Stella designs hand-knit sweaters, made from kooky colors and patterns. Rosetta showed me some pictures of them cut from a magazine.

The most exciting thing, though, is that they hang out with

the royal family! Rosetta says they got to know Prince Andrew when he was going to school in Lakefield, just north of here. Once the girls even brought him home for dinner!

"Horse shit." Hank launches a thin stream of tobacco juice into the cosmos.

"That's what I thought," I say, "but Rosetta sure made it sound legit. Told me what the menu was right down to the kind of pickles she served. The prince said her veal paprikash was even better than what they serve at Buckingham Palace. I asked her if she gave him real cloth napkins 'cause I heard that when the prince was at Lakefield, he saw paper napkins for the first time on a picnic and was so amazed he let them fly away in the wind. Rosetta said, 'The prince would never do such a thing. His manners were impeccable.'"

"Horse shit," Hank spits again. "If that woman's daughters are so hoity-toity, what's she doin' living here?"

I think about that for a minute. It's a good question. Why *don't* they take her back to England or at least set her up in a nicer place than this? Suddenly I'm not feeling so friendly toward those girls. What a couple of scammers! Raking in the dough from all their fancy clients and not sharing a cent with their poor ma in Canada. I was an idiot not to see it before!

I march back to Rosetta's room and knock, nice and loud. No answer. I'm getting madder by the minute, a real Savage Red mood. I can't believe they waited all this time to visit, only to stay for fifteen stinkin' minutes!

I barge in. Rosetta's alone, sound asleep with a smile on her face. Her nails are done, and her hair is twisted into a French roll with rosebuds and baby's breath tucked into the knot. I've never seen Rosetta asleep before. Her lips curl in, and I realize she's probably taken out her teeth. She wouldn't like me to see her like that. I figure I better leave and go be mad somewhere else.

But something makes me look again. Rosetta seems awful pale, as if the Savage Red nail polish sucked all the color out of her skin.

"Rosetta?"

"Rosetta?"

"ROSETTA!"

I'm afraid to touch her. What if she's . . . dead? But Rosetta'd have a fit if she knew I hollered for the nurses just 'cause she was sleeping peacefully. It's just Rosetta, I tell myself. Nothing to be scared of. And I touch her hand above the place where her twisted fingers disappear into the ball of fuzzy wool. Her hand's cold. Cold as stone. Cold as death.

I trip back from the bed. Dead! It's my turn to go cold. Suddenly it's hard to breathe. I gotta get out of this room! I run out the door . . . and slam right into Miss Knabb so hard she falls smack on the tile floor. She glares at me like I clobbered her on purpose and gets up wincing.

"Do you realize if you had knocked down one of our residents, they might have broken a hip or worse?"

Shit yeah! The guy who used to share Hank's room broke a hip, got pneumonia, and two weeks later he was dead!

Knabb's dill pickle face has got *accusation* written all over it. Her fingers are twitching, getting ready to point at me. She's not sure what I've done, but she's sure I've done something wrong. Why else would I come flying out like that? Why else would my tongue be so tied in knots I can't get a word out?

"Michelle . . . what is it?" Her every word's a picture. A Monopoly square: GO TO JAIL! GO DIRECTLY TO JAIL!

I killed her. That's what Knabb thinks. I killed Rosetta! For money, maybe, or jewelry. She'll have me searched, and when she doesn't find anything, she'll figure I've been taking stuff all along, and Rosetta found out so I held a pillow over her face till she stopped breathing.

The more the seconds tick by, the worse it looks, and still I stand there like a dope. Some inmates and nurses have stopped what they're doing and are edging down the hall. Knabb glances at Rosetta's door. Dr. Meyers walks up. Meyers! He's not just the doctor here. He's the coroner, too! The one who does the autopsies, who signs the papers, "Murder by pillow."

Meyers sees the storm brewing in Knabb's face and starts frowning, too. They must be in cahoots, those two! They reek of wine. So that's how they spend their lunch hours, plotting revenge on petty criminals like me!

Another picture pops into my head. I must be going crazy. This time what I see is a dark, smelly wine shop in Paris. Rosetta and her daughters are knitting and watching heads roll off a guillotine. ONE! Knabb's head. TWO! Dr. Meyers' head. THREE! Is it me? Am I number three? 'Cause suddenly I'm seeing everything sideways, from Rosetta's lap.

Then I realize what I am. I'm the ball of wool! Rosetta's fingers pull and twist and turn me around, and I hear her whisper, "If you don't like the ending, Michelle, make up a new one."

Suddenly I see my way out. The girls! "The girls were the last ones to see Rosetta alive, not me! If anyone did anything with pillows, it must've been the girls!"

"What are you talking about?" snaps Knabb.

"Her twins! Erika and Stella! They were just here!"

"Rosetta doesn't have any family."

"Does too! I saw them—" Uh-oh. Dr. Meyers is going in. He's gonna know.

"Michelle," says Knabb. "Stop talking nonsense. Twins? You mean her babies, who died?"

"Died?"

"Born and died on the same day at least fifty years ago. They're buried in the cemetery." She flicks a hand in the direction of the graveyard, which backs onto the nursing home. "I'm surprised Rosetta didn't tell you. She used to tell everyone about them."

I can't believe Rosetta would make it up. I can't believe she would lie to me. Was it a big joke to her? Let's see if we can scam the little scammer with an even bigger scam?!

Dr. Meyers comes out and whispers to Knabb. He's looking at me kind of sad as if he hasn't figured out the pillow angle yet, but Knabb doesn't need to see Rosetta to know I'm a danger to society.

"Michelle, sit on that chair and do not move until we come out. Do you hear?"

Oh I hear all right. I hear my cue to run. Leave behind that gotcha-now glare on Knabb's face and the poor-little-criminal smile on Dr. Meyers', run past the clumps of nurses and aides and whispering inmates, past the droning televisions and yackety-yak radios, past walkers and wheelchairs and nodding white heads, past smells of pee, perfume, powder and dinner, past the key pad without punching the code and out the back door—

*BZZZZZ . . .*

The alarm buzzes after me like an army of killer bees. I hurdle over Hank's rows of petunias and climb over the fence to the graveyard. I gotta find them. I gotta know.

Even if I wasn't feeling so scrambled, I couldn't miss their grave. They've got a huge mother of a gravestone, polished so smooth it shines like pink satin. On top is the stone castle with all its spires and turrets.

*Sweet Dreams, Our Darling Infant Girls.* It says their names, *Erika and Stella,* and the day they were born and died, *November 10, 1943.* Rosetta's fairy-tale king, Ludwig, is here, too. *Ludwig Alfred Teodosovich, born December 31, 1899, died December 31, 1943.*

So the stone castle was for all of them. And they were here the whole time, lying in the ground not a hundred feet from where Rosetta was lying in her bed. The way Rosetta talked, I thought Ludwig was buried far away in Europe or something. . . . Jeez, this says he died on his birthday, same year the girls died. I wonder what he died of. A broken heart? Did he kill himself or something? Poor Rosetta. . . .

Standing here with my hands around the castle spires, I'm not mad at Rosetta anymore. So what if she made it all up? It was real to *her*. She knew her girls would come and get her, 'cause she was the one making up her own ending.

But if that's what happened, why did *I* see them? Did I just *want* to see them? If Knabb had peeked through the crack in the door, would she have seen something totally different?

I lean my forehead against the cool pink stone. So much weird stuff happened today, I half expect it to talk to me, but it doesn't, not in any language.

Maybe it helps me anyway. I'm not scared anymore. My thoughts aren't racing around so fast. Back at the nursing home, I was too upset to think straight. Rosetta was ninety-three. That's old. Old people die. No one pressed a pillow to her face. She imagined her girls into being and let go of life.

Yeah right. . . . Knabb'll buy that!

I wish this whole awful day was a story. Then I could make up a different ending. Rosetta would be alive. Her twins would be real. I wouldn't have run away. . . .

It's not a story, though. I can't bring Rosetta to life. I can't make her twins real. But . . . I guess I could go back and tell Knabb the truth, as far as I know it. *Tell the Truth. Take Responsibility for my Actions* . . .

Maybe like the poor guy at the end of *A Tale of Two Cities,* I'll be offering up my head for the guillotine. But as I walk back to the nursing home, the twigs cracking under my heels sound just like the clicking of knitting needles. It's not a scary sound. It makes me feel like Rosetta's real close, wrapping a warm woolly sweater around my shoulders. And all of a sudden I'm sure, sure as if she told me herself, that Rosetta would like this ending. She'd like it just fine.

# (Frances)

Monday, August 9, 1993
The Rose Bed & Breakfast
Dun Laoghaire, Ireland

David MacDuff
Willow Glen Estates
Lee, Ontario
CANADA

Dear Duff,

As you can see, we are in Ireland way ahead of schedule—Dad's fault of course. He won't admit it, but I suspect there is a new movie idea percolating in his evil little brain. I recognize the signs: daydreaming, deafness, and the irritating habit of shuffling our—all right—*my* carefully laid plans.

None of this seems to bother Petra. She is truly Dad's daughter. In London the two of them tripped happily along, their heads in the smog, not paying attention to where they were going, and when they got us lost, they figured so much the better—adventure! It drove me CRAZY, especially when we're on such a tight schedule. Dad said, "What's the big deal, Fran? We got to see the important stuff, right? Westminster Abbey, where they crown the queens, Buckingham Palace, where they house the queens, and the Tower of London, where they chop off the queens' heads!" Only Dad could reduce several centuries of proud royal tradition to three short snappy scenes.

His obsession with films is turning this reunion trip into a bad remake of *Planes, Trains and Automobiles.* From London, we took a train to Holyhead, Wales, and then a ferry to Ireland. It might have been bearable if it hadn't rained the whole time and if an exhaustingly friendly Irish couple—Tess and Gravy—hadn't bombarded us continually with good cheer. They kept calling Dad "brilliant" because he could guzzle his Guinness and still talk sensibly (of course, that's "sensibly" according to Gravy) and they kept calling Petra "Pet" and exclaiming how adorable she was. Me, they couldn't figure out.

"Sisters, are ye?" asked Gravy. "But yer nothin' alike!"

"You're telling me," I was tempted to say, but instead I explained that Petra and I are half sisters and that's why she has fair skin, blonde curls and blue eyes, while I look like a Greek fisherman. "Petra takes after Dad," I said, while she stole a sip of Gravy's Guinness.

"That she does, that she does!" he laughed. Petra hugged and kissed him with her moustache of Guinness foam.

"You're brilliant, Gravy!" she cried.

Tess just laughed. "She's for the men, that one!"

You know, David, she's right. Six years old, and Petra has men figured out. I'm sixteen, and I can't even talk to my own father.

Since they were treating me like a bump on a log anyway, I decided to act like one and sat there updating the lists in my travel journal. I'm keeping track of mileage, travelers' cheque numbers, and facts I want to remember. Dad made a big joke of it to Tess and Gravy.

"Don't you think Frances should loosen up a little?" he said. "Journals are supposed to be fun!" Right. This from the man who smashes bottles when the current draft of his screenplay isn't going well.

"My travel journal is not for *fun,*" I told him. "It's an account book."

"You can have fun writing a grocery list," he said. "Just embellish with a bit of the ol' blarney, eh, Gravy?"

"I don't write *fiction,* Dad," I said. "Fiction is for liars."

"Ah. Like me, you mean."

Well, he said it, I didn't.

So far Ireland looks about as promising as our father–daughter relationship. People say how green Ireland is, but everything I've seen so far is grey. Grey sky, grey water, grey sidewalks peppered with dog poop. It's depressingly rainy here, just as it was in England. I wonder, if Dad had chosen a sunny place for this reunion, would we get along better? Would we run to each other in slow motion and fall into a loving father–daughter embrace? Probably not.

Even amidst all this greyness, Dad and Petra find ways to have fun. They scampered off awhile ago to find the toilet in our B&B. It's the first thing they do wherever we stay. Perhaps by the end of this trip I'll understand their fascination with foreign plumbing.

As for me, I plan to curl up in bed with the poem you slipped into my pocket at the airport. It's so beautiful, David. Thank-you.

Love,

Frances

Thursday, August 12, 1993
"The Westbury"
Dublin

David MacDuff
Willow Glen Estates
Lee, Ontario
CANADA

Dear David,

Don't get used to me being at this address because we're moving again. ARRGH! Just when I was starting to feel settled in this hotel and was looking forward to watching Oksana's film shoot, Dad changed the plans again.

Did I tell you that one of our reasons for coming to Dublin was to see Oksana? It's not like me to forget, but my brain is feeling as scrambled as our itinerary. I was really looking forward to seeing her work. In the nine years she and Dad have been married, this is the first film shoot I've seen. Oksana is usually good to have around, too, as a buffer between Dad and me. This time, though, she wasn't her usual bubbly self, maybe because of the role she's playing: a punk rock singer trying to make amends with her lesbian hooker mother who has taken up the classical violin. Phew! I doubt even Dad could dream up something so insane. Just once, in either fact or fiction, wouldn't it be comforting to come across a normal family?

Making movies, I've concluded, involves a lot of waiting around and drinking coffee. They spent the entire day filming one scene— a drugged-out sequence with three drag queens spraying walls with graffiti. Petra told the actors that when she was little, she used to paint on walls, too. The next thing you know, they've got her up on one of the actors' shoulders spray painting the top of the wall. Once again, my adorable half sister was the hit of the party.

It was the same thing at the pub we went to after the filming. Dad, Oksana and the crew were discussing obscure road movies that I've never seen. Petra was showing her new pal, the bartender, how to make an egg stand on one end. Another party where I didn't belong. What I really wanted to do was crawl down and check out the flagstone floors. *Real* stone floors, David! Two hundred years old, the waitress told me. If you had been there, we might have done it, slipped under the table when no one was looking. But you weren't there, and I started thinking about the Guinness spills and dog poop residue and other unmentionables that were probably on the floor, so I stayed in my seat.

After an eternity Dad and Oksana rounded up Petra and joined me at the table. For once they looked serious and said that they had an announcement to make. Oh David. I was sure I knew what they were going to say: another divorce.

But Pet shrieked, "YOU'RE GONNA HAVE A BABY, AREN'T CHA?!"

All conversation around us died. I don't know which was worse, thinking I might have another half sister on the way or enduring the stares of fifty half-drunk strangers.

"Sorry, folks," Oksana laughed. "There's no baby." Someone shouted "Try, try again, luv!" And everyone (except me) guffawed.

People turned back to their own conversations and Dad cleared his throat. "Girls, what would you think of a road trip? We'll rent a car and explore the countryside, just the three of us, while Oksana finishes filming. It'll be great! What do you say?" He phrased it as a question, but didn't give us a choice.

So it's to be *Planes, Trains and Automobiles, Part 2* and the plan (if you can call it a plan) is to rent a car tomorrow and head north. Dad will drive, I will navigate and Pet will sit quietly in the back seat (HA!).

Miss you, Duff!

Frances

TRAVEL JOURNAL OF FRANCES M. REID

Friday the 13th, August 1993
Somewhere in County Meath

*The Road Trip, Day One*

Number of rental cars rejected by Dad on the basis of not being "cool" enough: 6

Number of times going roundabout the roundabouts: 69

Number of times Dad drove on the wrong side of the road: 99

Number of wrong turns taken: 492

Number of times my advice was silenced by Dad's creative swear words: 6 + 69 + 99 + 492 = 666

666.

That about sums up the day. Devilish.

Saturday, August 14, 1993
County Louth, Ireland

David MacDuff
Willow Glen Estates
Lee, Ontario
CANADA

Dear David,
Today, for the first time, I felt old Ireland. It crept up behind me, tapped me on the shoulder and whispered in my ear, "Welcome home."

I'm *not* home. There's not a speck of Irish blood in me. But something happened today. Maybe it was the haunting music I heard on the car radio before Dad made me put on something more "lively."

"Aren't we a pair," he laughed. "My kid likes uillean pipes and I like U2."

We were looking for a stone tomb called the Proleek Dolmen, and I had the route nicely planned, but Dad kept pulling us off track every time we passed a pretty lane or tumbledown ruin. It was noon by the time we pulled into a cottage pub called The Shepherd's Rest. Wouldn't you know, there were three drunken shepherds resting inside. It was heartwarming how glad they were to see us.

"Hello!" they slurred. "Sit ye doon! What brings ye to these godforsaken parts?"

Once they discovered that Petra's mother is an American movie star and that Dad once coached a Canadian hockey team (even if it was just the Lee Lions), I knew Dad and Petra would be stuck there for a while. So when the barmaid brought some sandwiches to the table, I excused myself and took lunch outside. She whispered as I left, "Here's a Fanta Lemon and crisps for ye, luv. Don't mind the fellas. They're excited to see someone new."

Outside, the misty rain had stopped. A few ropes of light swung down through cracks in the grey clouds, and a perfect rainbow shimmered and stretched over the hill behind the cottage. I decided to follow it to the top of the hill and see if I could spot the Dolmen from up there.

As I picked my way up the steep wooded path, I could no longer see the rainbow, but had the feeling that I had stepped *into* it, and it was now a rainbow all of green—from the yellow-green leaves rustling overhead to the black-green moss crouching on logs beside the path.

At the top of the hill, I was startled by a tall standing stone. At first I thought it was a man standing still among the trees. Then I saw two other stones lying beside it, radiating outward, half-buried in the ground. Strangely they were warm to the touch, not cold as I expected.

Then I did something that will surprise you, David. It surprised me! I put my arms around the standing stone . . . and hugged it. *You* know I'm not a "huggy" person, and there was no logical reason for me to hug that stone except that I was alone and happy and wanted to and maybe that's reason enough. Dad would have been proud of me, doing something so illogical. Too bad he'll never know.

Love,

Frances

Monday, August 16, 1993 # Carrick-a-Rede, County Antrim, Northern Ireland

Calm, Frances. Be calm. Write something. No. If I tried writing now, I'd shred the paper with my pen. Jab, rip, tear, dig . . . Control, Frances. Self-control. That's what makes us civilized. Hmmm . . . civilized like those people who survive plane crashes in remote areas by eating each other. I wonder if those bodies-who-became-lunch weren't really dead to start with. Maybe they were so obnoxious that murder and cannibalism became justifiable options for their fellow travelers. Hmm . . . I wonder. . . .

Patricide is when you kill your father. What's it called when you kill your daughter? Is there a word for that? Not that Dad was actually trying to kill us I suppose, but he came pretty close, driving so fast along that roller coaster of a road. Dad and Petra squealed like pigs the whole time. I'm surprised Dad didn't take his hands off the wheel and hold them over his head like Petra was doing. Crazy road. The shoulder dropped almost straight down to the sea, and there wasn't a fence in sight to keep us safe. Safe! At the speed Dad was driving? Not a chance.

Every time I yelled, "Slow down!" Dad said I sounded like my mother and turned up the volume on the radio. So I tried yelling, "Slow, please, loose chippings!"

That was a road sign I saw the first day, warning people to slow down on gravel roads. I put it on the list of Road Signs to Remember in my journal. I don't know why I liked it so much—maybe because when I'm around Dad my self-control starts skidding around as if it's on a gravel road. But yelling, "Slow, please, loose chippings!" didn't slow Dad down. He just said, "Now you sound like an Irish mother."

As if his driving wasn't nauseating enough, Dad insisted on stopping at Carrick-a-Rede to try crossing its famous rope bridge. Bridge! I've seen string bikinis that look more sturdy than that glorified piece of dental floss swinging above the sea. Once you get to the tiny island at the other end, there's nothing to do but turn around and cross back. Two heart attacks for the price of one. There was a huge lineup of crazy people waiting to get on it, though.

"All they need is a car ride with you, Dad," I said. "You guys go ahead. I'll stay here."

"Frances, *dear,*" he replied. "Could you try to be a pleasant human being for an hour or so and come with us?"

"No," I said.

Petra was pulling on Dad's arm. She couldn't wait to get on the bridge. Dad lowered his voice.

"Could you at least *try* this for Pet? She wants to look up to you."

Boy, that ticked me off! As if there aren't other things that she could admire me for.

"Maybe she'd like to look up to you, too, Dad. She *could* if you'd start acting like a father instead of a child!" Dad looked at me as if he wondered how he could have spawned this alien offspring.

I suppose he has forgotten The Time Before, when he was an ordinary guy, a passably good father, teaching at the Lee High School. Before Oksana breezed into town to film that low-budget horror, *You Never Know,* and Dad started hanging around the crew like a dumb overage groupie, pestering Oksana to read the screen-play he scribbled away at when he could have been spending time with Mom and me. Then came the awful day that stalker tried to shoot Oksana and hit poor Alex Meyers instead, and whose side did Dad rush to? Not Alex's, oh no. He went straight to Oksana.

Did he wonder how *I* was, his six-year-old child at home? I *knew* Alex. We'd both been in the mock royal wedding they staged at the high school the year before. Alex was Princess Anne. She helped me into my flower girl dress, told me how adorable I looked. Me! Ugly little Frances! Adorable! Alex was so beautiful, I was in awe of her. The same way Dad was in awe of Oksana, I suppose.

Oksana said she fell in love with Dad's writing before she fell in love with the man. I'm astounded that she fell in love with either.

Dad, you stride across that rope bridge with such confidence. You think it will never collapse? No. You believe in the bridge. Well, watch out, Dad. Don't take it for granted. Because some-times bridges give up. And so do daughters.

August 17, 1993,
2:00 am
Heather Farm,
Giant's Causeway,
County Antrim

David MacDuff
Willow Glen Estates
Lee, Ontario
CANADA

David,

What I wouldn't give to be standing next to you, skipping stones into the pond on Leebrook Road. Skip, skip, skip, plop—

our problems sink to the bottom. Everything seems so much easier at home. Here, I'm no better than a bunch of loose chippings.

Tonight, my father told me to f—k off. Or, more precisely, to F—K OFF!

How *could* he, David? How could *anyone* tell their own daughter to—well, therein lies the reason, I suppose. He doesn't see me as his daughter.

I'm so mortified. He said it right in front of perfect strangers, not to mention Petra. You'd think that even if he hated me, he would try to protect her, the daughter he does love.

Can I tell you about it, David? Maybe it will help. . . .

I guess we'd been bugging each other all day, and it was already late when we got to our B&B. Dad said he needed a drink. The lady who runs the place, Mrs. O'Brien, said we also needed some freshly baked trout which her husband had caught this afternoon. Have you ever been served fish with the head still attached, David? It's truly horrifying to eat something that is watching you. I had to cover my trout's head with a piece of lettuce before I could eat a bite.

During dinner, Mrs. O'Brien told us about the Giant's Causeway, where we planned to hike tomorrow. She said according to legend, the giant Finn MacCool built the causeway with stepping stones so he could cross the sea to Scotland.

Another guest joined us about then, a blonde, American, forty-something floozy who was already half-drunk and could hardly keep her hands off Dad. When she found out who Dad was, she shifted her flirting into high gear. "Ooo! You wrote that movie? That's one of my favorites! Really! Ooo! You're married to Oksana Riker? I'm such a big fan. . . ." Every time Dad poured himself a drink, the floozy said, "Ooo, that's my favorite. I'll have one, too!" Dad lapped it up, David! It was so disgusting.

"It's time we got Pet to bed, Dad," I said.

"She's havin' fun," he slurred.

"We have a big day tomorrow. I think we should all get to bed."

Dad and the floozy thought that was a big joke. "Maybe we should, eh?" said Dad. "Nudge, nudge, wink, wink." They laughed so hard they almost choked. I wished they had. I was tired. Tired of being the grown-up. Tired of my father and Pet and the whole stupid trip.

"You make me sick," I whispered.

The floozy giggled. I guess she thought it was another joke. Dad looked as if he wasn't sure. I stood at the door. "C'mon, Pet. Now."

"Stay here, Pet," said Dad. "Frances will be a bad influence on you, turn you against me."

"The only bad influence in this room is you, Dad."

"My darling Frances. Please pull the pickle out of your ass."

I'd heard enough. Mixed as my feelings are for Petra, I wasn't about to subject her to that. I pushed her through the door.

" 'Night Daddy," she yawned.

Behind our backs, Dad muttered to the floozy, "Frances thinks I'm the world's worst f—king father."

That's when I lost it, David. Skidded right out of control. In front of all those people—Dad, the floozy, Mrs. O'Brien and Pet—I said, "You may be the world's worst father, but I'm sure you do just fine in the 'effing' department. You could win an award. Most Female Partners in One Pathetic Lifetime."

Finally the floozy stopped giggling. Dad stared at me. "F—k off, Frances," he said. "Just. F—K OFF!"

I hurried Pet upstairs and got her into her pajamas. The whole time, Dad's words blasted through my brain. "F—k off!" My own father told me to f—k off!

I heard the front door slam and looked out the window. Dad was striding across the lane to our rental car. The floozy had him by the arm. He shook his head, snapped something at her and sped off, tires squealing. David, he'd been *drinking!* He's out there now on those crazy roads after dark. He'll get himself arrested or killed or worse—he'll kill someone else. Unless the floozy manages to stop him, I suppose. She went roaring off after him in her own car.

That was around 11:30. Pet was already half-asleep when I got her into bed. I've been up most of the time waiting, but I did drift off once, and David, I had the strangest dream. I wish there weren't an ocean between us, so I could talk to you about it.

In the dream, Dad, Petra and I were eating dinner in a castle that belonged to the giant Finn MacCool. It was a drafty, dangerous place perched on the edge of a cliff. Through the cracks in the walls, I could hear the sea below rumbling like a great hungry stomach. Mrs. MacCool served us stew out of a round stone bowl. The broth was black as night, and when I stirred it up, fish heads and eyeballs rolled to the surface. Petra devoured her soup as if it were chocolate, but Dad was ignoring his. He was too busy arguing with Finn about the best auto route from Dublin to the north shore.

I knew they were both wrong. I'd planned our route to the north coast, after all. But they wouldn't listen to me. I was so mad, I began to shake. The table began to shake, too, and I wasn't sure if I had started it or if Finn had. He'd begun pounding on the table with his boulder-sized fists. Then the walls began to tremble. Dust and pebbles fell from the ceiling. I shouted at Dad and Finn to stop arguing, but still they ignored me. Since they couldn't hear me yelling, I tried singing instead, "Slow, please, loose chippings. SLOW, PLEASE, LOOSE CHIPPINGS—" Finally they looked at me just as the far end of the castle collapsed and tumbled off the cliff, taking Petra with it, then Mrs. MacCool, then Finn, then Dad, his eyes wild with fear. . . .

I woke up still trembling. Petra was curled up beside me, her sweaty forehead pressed against my shoulder. As I stared down at her, the horror of my dream washed over me again. Oh David. The horror was—do I dare even write this down? The horror was . . . that when I saw Petra disappear over the edge of the cliff, I was relieved. Happy. Thrilled! As if an annoying little problem had just gone *skip, skip, skip, plop* to the bottom of the sea. I don't know how I felt about losing Dad. I think I felt . . . nothing. Nothing.

I probably won't mail this, David. I'll burn it or seal it and stick it in the back of my journal. You know me better than anyone, but even you didn't know what dark thoughts lurked inside me. I didn't know it myself.

Frances

Tuesday, August 17, 1993 # Heather Farm, Giant's Causeway, County Antrim

My mother raised me to be a sensible person. I've never believed in extrasensory perception. In my experience, there's always a logical explanation for unusual phenomena. But today that belief cracked just a bit, and some of the old Irish magic shone through. . . .

Dad staggered in at 3:00 A.M. and collapsed on his bed without saying a word. In the morning he was hung over and subdued. We talked to Petra, but not to each other. I was extra nice to Petra, trying to make up for the dream, I suppose. I read her a storybook about Finn MacCool that Mrs. O'Brien brought up this morning. I think Mrs. O'Brien wanted to make sure we were all alive and well. She tried to coax me down for breakfast. "We serve the best Ulster Fry in the County Antrim!" she insisted. I said I wasn't hungry, but the real reason was that I couldn't face the other guests after last night.

She asked if we were going to see the ruins of the Dunluce

Castle on the cliff top just down the road. My ears perked up when I heard *cliff top*. I asked her to tell me about it. She said that the castle was added onto over the years and may have been expanded just a bit too much because one day a chunk of it slid over the edge and tumbled into the sea. I got goose bumps when she told me that, but I assumed I must have heard her talking about it last night or maybe read about it in our guide book.

When I stepped outside the B&B, I was amazed. It was dusk when we arrived last night, so I had no idea what a treasure we had stumbled upon. If there is such a place as heaven, then surely a corner of it must be called Heather Farm. There is every color of flower in Mrs. O'Brien's garden, and growing along the hedges are wild fuschias with plump red blossoms. Surrounding the farm are green and purple fields where the grazing sheep and cows seem oblivious to the beauty that is all around them. Beyond the cows is a fence, beyond that is the high path of the Giant's Causeway and beyond that—a drop of a hundred feet or more to the rocks and the pounding sea below.

I've seen pictures of the Giant's Causeway in books at home and slides of it in Geography class. It looks like a giant honeycomb and stretches all along the coast and even under the sea to Scotland. It was formed when lava seeped through a crack in the earth's crust and crystallized when it hit the water. But pictures couldn't have prepared me for the real thing. It was . . . otherworldly. If I could have hugged the whole place, I would have.

"I know how you like rocks. I thought we'd stay put for a few days and poke around." These were the first words Dad had spoken directly to me all morning. He seemed proud of remembering my interest in geology.

We walked from the B&B to the Giant's Causeway Visitors Center, where Petra and I watched the film about the history of the place. Dad excused himself and came back ten minutes later carrying two bags from the gift shop. That was so like Dad, I thought. I remember when he and Mom would fight, Dad would storm out of the house only to appear several hours later with an expensive bouquet of flowers for Mom. Years later Mom told me that she wished he had just apologized or at least talked to her.

Petra's gift from Dad was a little Irish flute called a tin whistle. Played properly, it sounds lovely. Played by Petra, it sounded like a sick seagull. I think I know what Dad's motive was. The recorder was my instrument in public school. I gave it up years ago, but Dad wouldn't know that.

My gift from dad was a bumpy rust-colored stone.

"It's a geode," he said. "Or it might be one. The girl said it's a lottery. Break it open and you might find crystal treasure inside."

"Or you might not?" I said.

Pet skipped ahead of us, blowing on her tin whistle. Dad cleared his throat.

"Frances, you know something? You're like that stone."

"Thank-you, but I see no resemblance."

"See that's just what I mean. Sixteen years old and you're crusty as an old—No. Let me try to say this right. You've built up walls around yourself, Frances, and they're hard as rock."

So we're back to it being my fault, I thought.

"—but I'm pretty sure, Frances, that just like this geode, there's something special inside you."

"Aren't you taking a risk, Dad?" I said. "What if we crack this open and find it empty?"

What could he say? He's the one who set us up for failure. I put the stone in my pocket, and we walked in silence to fetch Pet.

The Giant's Causeway had two paths, a "high road" and a "low road." The towering rock wall of columns stretching vertically between them was home to hundreds of swooping squawking seabirds. The sky was undecided—half-blue, half-grey. Now and then a few drops of rain fell. We decided to walk along the high path first while the view was still clear and return along the lower path later. The high path was narrow—no railings again—so we walked single file with Petra leading the way, still blowing on her tin whistle.

"You're the Pied Piper, Pet!" I said. "See if you can coax those people below to follow us." But no one came. Except for us, the high path was deserted.

Behind me Dad said, "Still mad, Frances?"

"Yes, if you must know."

"Why?"

*Why?* Did he think the gift of a stone could change everything? Why was I mad?! Where would he like me to start? Drinking and driving! Acting like a three-year-old instead of a responsible adult! Screwing around on my mother! And maybe now, screwing around on Oksana! There was too much to say, so I said nothing.

"I know I've been preoccupied," he said. "It's this idea I have for a movie."

I knew it. I saw the signs. It's beyond Dad's capabilities to be both a father and a writer at the same time.

"It's a road movie . . ."

I remembered Dad quizzing the film crew about road movies back in Dublin. *Five Easy Pieces. Highway 61. Fandango. Thelma and Louise.*

"Haven't there been enough road movies, Dad?"

"Not like this one. It's got two characters who are so different sparks fly when they're in the same country, let alone in the same car. A grandad and his grandson. The old guy's a free-wheeling rock n' roller type, and the kid's a real prude—"

"I am not!"

"I wasn't talking about you! It's a movie, Frances. Fiction."

"It *is* us."

"Absolutely not . . . Maybe it was *inspired* by us, but it's not the same story at all—"

"That's the real reason for this road trip isn't it? Research! You put us in that car like lab rats in a maze."

"I put us in that car so we'd be a family."

"Dad, forced proximity does not a family make."

"Okay wait. Just wait," he said. "We always do this. Start out talking and end up pissed off with each other and—"

"And then you tell me to f. off."

"I'm sorry about that, okay? Don't tell me you've led such a sheltered life that you've never heard those two words before."

"Of course I have. I just never expected to hear them from my own father."

"Once again, Frances, child of my loins, I am sorry. Okay? Good. Now can I tell you my other idea? This one *is* about us."

"I'm listening."

"I thought if we had a code word, something we could say when one of us starts pushing the other's mad buttons, something to make us step back and see if we can solve the problem before we get too mad . . ."

A code word, I thought. Not a bad idea. A word or phrase I could say when Dad starts being obnoxious . . . I knew just the thing. When Dad pushes my mad buttons, as he calls them, when I feel as though bits of me might fly off in all directions—

"How about 'Slow, please, loose chippings' as our code?" I said.

"Perfect," Dad smiled. I smiled back. And then we heard Petra scream.

While Dad and I were talking, we had slowed to a stop, and Pet had skipped on ahead. I hadn't realized quite how far ahead, until I heard her terrified squeal and saw her blonde curls disappear over the edge.

PET! My God, *PET!*

The first thing I felt was fury at myself and Dad for not keeping her safe. Then quick as an avalanche, the anger evaporated and left behind fear. Sickening, nauseating, horrifying fear.

"PET!" I screamed. I ran. I didn't care that the path was narrow. I didn't care that pebbles spun out from under my feet and fell *chip-chip-chip* to the rocks below.

I couldn't see her, but I could hear her voice, small and scared, and not far away. Irrationally I thought she was already an angel. I dropped to my stomach and peered over the edge. Pet was crouched on a ledge several feet below me, her face white with fear. Both of her hands were clamped around a jutting rock. Her knuckles were scratched and beaded with blood.

Suddenly I was back in the dream in Finn MacCool's castle. Pet was over the edge, but this time I had a chance to save her.

"Oh Pet. Thank God."

"Frances, I'm scared," she whispered.

"Pet, give me your hand."

Her hand felt tiny in mine, clammy and slippery. I couldn't hold on! Quickly I grabbed her wrist. That was better.

"Pet, don't worry. I won't let you fall."

Her eyes were huge. I never noticed before the flecks of gold mixed in with the blue. My father's eyes.

Pet was looking at me as if I were all the world, and for that moment, I suppose I was. I was all that stood between her and safety. I suddenly realized how selfish I had been. All this time when I was being mad at Dad and sorry for myself, I hadn't been thinking about Pet at all. She was just an annoying bug, an interloper, the daughter for Dad that I could never be. But maybe Pet wanted something, too. Maybe that's why she was always trying to play with my hair and why she always snuggled up to me in bed. Maybe she wanted . . . a sister.

Fortunately my logical inner voice yelled to the rest of my scrambled-egg brain: *What she needs right now is for you to pull her up!* For that, I needed help.

"Dad, where are you?!" I yelled.

"Here," he whispered. He was standing beside me in shock. He was looking down at Pet, tears streaming down his cheeks. "You're alive," he whispered.

"Dad, she's fine. Just help me to pull her up." He lay down beside me. Pet slowly let go of the rock and gave him her other hand.

"Pull!" I said. "Again!"

It was a tug of war between us and the cliff face. Pet was the rope and the prize. We pulled her by the wrists, the arms, the jacket, until finally she was safe on the path. We shuffled back as far as we could and sat there, a tangled pile of arms and legs.

Dad was still in shock. He was patting both our heads and kissing our cheeks. Pet squeezed me so hard. I've never been hugged like that before. Then she looked at me very earnestly and said, "Thank-you Frances. I love you."

How could a person resist that? I hugged her back.

Then Pet started to laugh of all things, a little nervous giggle, and Dad started laughing, too. That's all we need, I thought. Hysteria brought on by trauma. I was feeling a bit hysterical myself.

"*What* on earth are you two laughing about?" Didn't they realize that Pet almost died?

"I was just thinking," Dad laughed, "they need a sign here that says—"

We all finished his sentence together: "Slow, please, loose chippings!"


Pet fell asleep early tonight, exhausted from the excitement and the long careful walk home. Dad and I were tired, too, but we decided to watch the sun set from the front step of our B&B. We were surrounded by color so vibrant, it almost hurt to look at it—the pink and orange of the sky, the deep green of the fields, the black and white line of Holsteins as they wound their way home on the cow path.

"You were great today, Frances," said Dad.

"Pet's a good kid," I replied.

"So are you. I was wondering . . . did you crack open your geode yet?"

He knew it was still in my pocket. I wasn't sure I wanted to look inside. I was remembering my dream and the round stone bowl of Mrs. MacCool's that was filled with hideous surprises.

"It won't be easy to crack, Dad. I'll need a hammer."

"No problem. I'll get one from Mrs. O'Brien." When he came back, I held the hammer in one hand and the rock in the other. I took a deep breath. I placed the rock on a flagstone and tapped it gently.

"Come on! Give it a good whack!" Dad urged, hanging over my shoulder.

"Dad," I warned. "Slow, please, loose chippings!"

A few rough brown chips did fly off before it finally cracked open. What was inside wasn't exactly crystalline treasure, but it *was* interesting. Layer upon layer of smooth white mounds that looked like tiny, puffy clouds trapped inside the rock. It was beautiful in its way. I looked up to find Dad smiling at me.

"Told you so," he said.

(David)

## If Only

Frances,
you say we live
in a glacial landscape.
Patiently, passionately,
you paint with words
a picture of slow time
when mile-high ice
smothered these hills,
crushed trees,
chewed up boulders,
and spit them out
like seeds from a watermelon.
What I see in the hills is
the sweep of your hand,
the tilt of your smile,
the curve of your back.
What I see in the ice is my grandfather.
What I see in the chewed up bit of stone is me.
Today, Gramps arrives from Scotland.
Today, I will try to stay whole.
But, Frances, how much easier it would be
if only you were here.

## Acid

I scrub the toilet
(Mom's desperate request)
for the arrival of Mr. Clean.
The stains aren't our fault—
our water is hard—
but so is Gramps:
    *Dirrrt in yer house is like dirrrt in yer soul!*
I kill the stains finally with acid.
Acid, I know.
Stomach acid.
There's a rave rumbling
in my gut right now
in honor of His Majesty's visit.
Bits of food morph into devils,
cute little turds with horns
that kick-kick-kick off the sides,
and do the butterfly stroke.
Every kick, every stroke
feels like a knife in my gut.
But at least the bathroom is clean.

## Special Occasions

Remember, Frances,
when my gut did its thing
eleven years ago?
We were a matched set,
page boy and flower girl,
bookends at the mock royal wedding.
Greatest Show on Earth!
(or in Lee, anyway;
even the mayor was there!)
I had guests, too, inside my gut:
Billy Bile, Patty Puke, and the Butterfly Boys.
Miss Twitchit planned for every
catastrophe, calamity, contingency,
except me.
She didn't know
one small, shy page boy would be her downfall.
Inside my gut,
the guests raged to come out
and out they came
all over the stage,
the royal red carpet,
the spit 'n' shine polish of Prince Charming's shoes.
Backstage, Frances,
you held my head.
Petals from your hair fell in my lap.
You made me better
by being near.
Of course you remember, Frances,
but here's something you don't know:
Even though you wore that pretty dress,
I saw you in armor
and wished that I
could be that strong.

## Portrait of Frances

Since you left,
when my stomach starts to boil
I think of you in Ireland
lying on a cool green hill.
It's the best medicine.

## Round One—The Warm-up

I don't know why I fought with Mom.
I wasn't really mad at her, or Bri,
though we're all short-tempered
from lack of sleep.
Briana has colic.
I didn't know an eight-pound human
could cry so loud,
but maybe the smaller we are
the louder we need to cry—
otherwise, how would anyone hear?
Instead of crying I slam things,
like the front door.
And though it keeps me from crying,
it gets Mom started.
She's crumpled now on the floor inside,
face buried in an old tea towel
with Scotch thistles bristling all over it,
a gift from Gramps' last visit.
(In return for making life hell
he gives a tea towel,
and an ugly one at that.)
I want to say, "Slam it, Mom!
Ball it up, and slam it!"
But what I say instead is "Sorry,"
and guess what, Frances?
That works, too.

## See Dick Run

With every pump of my legs
I feel the poison leave my stomach.
I'm cycling to the store
to get currants for the Spotted Dick.
What a name for a pudding!
Just imagine its inventor—
an itchy old Brit with VD!
But it's Gramps' favorite dessert;
Mom always makes it his first night.
So currants I will get, plus vanilla and coffee.
Ten bucks in my pocket,
three things on my list,
but what I really have is FREEDOM!
At least, for now.
I feel this way every time I leave our new house,
where once there lived a girl who died.
Alex.
She was there, too,
a Princess—Anne—
the first time my stomach did its thing.
"Poor kid," she laughed.
She always laughed,
but now she's dead and
I sleep
or try to sleep
down the hall from her turret bedroom,
the bedroom Mom said I could have if I wanted,
but why would I want
to surround myself with death
when there's already so much inside me?

## The Dream

You know something of my nightmare, Frances,
but only what I chose to tell you.
You know there's a red beach
under a red sky
and you and my family are picnicking on the sand.
Our marshmallows ooze and plop into the fire.
We laugh.
Then the water starts
pulsing, churning, mounting.
Tidal wave!
I scream, "RUN!"
but we can't.
The sand is quicksand.
Flopping, breathless creatures
left behind by the water
writhe and twist,
smoke rising from their flesh.
The water is acid!
When it crashes down on you,
I see your skin and flesh and bones and
everything that is Frances
disappear in a puff of smoke
and I am left alone to wonder:
Why? Why?
Why was I spared?

**Me**

I realize something so obvious it hurts.
The beach in the dream
is my stomach.
The acid is mine.
I made it.
I did it.
Maybe I've always known,
but wouldn't admit it
to me
or you
or anyone
that I watched you die
and couldn't help.

## Wishing

In our subdivision,
streets are smooth as a man's shaved head,
grass is soft as peach fuzz,
trees are cut, new ones planted,
all to someone's careful plan.
But beyond the last lamppost,
before Leebrook Road,
everything changes.
Tangled trees bend over
a patched and potholed road.
Time slows down.
A daisy peeks up from a pothole
and I wish I could rescue it
like once I rescued a turtle
that was crossing this road.
Today, I remember the other lamppost
in the book you made me read
about the lion, the witch, and the wardrobe.
As long as the kids kept
the lamppost in sight
they could go back to their world,
but if they lost sight of it,
the danger (the thrill)
was they might never get back.
I think today
if I got lost
I might—I *would*—
be happy.

## Believing

I stop to throw stones
in the pond at the day care
where you and I, Frances, first became friends.
When Mom was working
and mornings were rushed.
Kiss, hug, and throw me in the door.
Then time slowed down.
Jewel would lay out
puzzles and playdough,
or take us hiking around the pond.
We'd call to the bear in the woods,
and wave to the chipmunks,
and you'd tell us how these hills
were once covered with ice.
The others thought you were making a story,
but Jewel believed you,
and I believed you.
I guess not everyone can imagine
what the eyes can't see.

## Anger

Jewel taught us to skip stones
when we're mad. She said,
"Imagine your anger into the stone,
throw it hard,
and watch it *skip-skip-skip-*PLOP!
right to the bottom of the pond."
I still do this.
Sometimes, it actually works.

## The Stone

I found a stone
or it found me.
Pressed against the toe of my shoe,
just asking to be thrown.
Smooth and black,
with blood red spots
and a hole in one end.
I imagined my anger—
at nightmares, stomachs,
the absence of friends,
the visits of grandfathers—
I imagined it all
into the stone
and threw it hard.
It fell at my feet.
If you were here, Frances,
you'd explain about magnetic pulls of the earth,
or my subconscious willing me to drop it,
or some such thing,
but, Frances, I know I threw that stone away
and it didn't want to go.

## Break Before Round Two

Back home
with currants, vanilla, coffee,
and a smooth, black stone in my pocket.
Nice as she can, Mom
suggests I wash up
and change my shirt.
Nice as I can, I say, "Sure."
No more fights today,
at least, between us.
We need to present a solid front.

**Heat**

I know it's here somewhere
in my junk drawer:
guitar picks, golf tees, coins—
here it is: a piece of leather thong.
Through the hole, tie a knot,
around my neck it goes.
The stone feels good,
cool on my chest,
because inside,
behind the grate of my ribs
a fire is burning.


**The Arrival**

Outside with Dad,
the glacier is here.
The rumble crunch of his voice
climbs to my window.
Though I can't hear the words
I don't need to,
I've got more than enough to remember him by:

 *Will you look at the wee laddie! Is this the runt, and yer hidin'
the rest of the litter? . . . Are ye gagged, lad? Get yer mouth out o' yer
collar and speak up! . . .*

 *Was I sleepin' through the tornado that swept through yer room,
Davy? It's shameful how ye throw yer things about. Get organized,
lad, or ye'll no get far in this life!*

Think of the stone,
think of the stone,
think of the stone.

## Masks

I've learned how to be
someone I'm not
by pulling on an invisible costume
and zipping it tight.
That way, I can be a lion, or a witch, or a wardrobe . . .
Now, who will I be for Gramps?
I am the lion,
but the appearance of Gramps
throws me off
and I almost forget my lines.
Gramps is not himself either.
The glacier has receded
and so has his hair.
He's not the wall of ice I remember.
He smiles, says *Good to see ye, Davy.*
Can so much have changed in two years?
Have I changed, too?

## Waiting

I carry his two bags.
   *They're not too much for ye, lad?*
No, I say.
I'm strong as a lion,
even though my arms
feel ready to fall off.
Crouched in the upstairs hall
I watch them talk below,
fuss and coo over Bri.
So far
the boxing match has been too easy.
I am suspicious,
waiting
for the surprise punch.

## The Hag Stone

Footsteps.
Gramps!
When I scramble to my feet,
the stone swings out.
  *What have ye there, Davy?*
  *A hag stone!*
A what? I say.
  *I'll wash up and then tell ye.*
I wait in my room
for the lecture, sermon, speech.
That's always been the way Gramps talks.
He talks, I listen,
and God help me
if I yawn.
He returns, still wearing that smile.
I wonder why?
It makes me nervous.
  *Now then, the hag stone,* says Gramps
and what he tells
is not a sermon or lecture or speech.
It's a story, a true one.

  *I was ten when I found a stone like the one round yer neck. 'Twas a bad time, Davy. My mother had died not long before, and I'd seen it happen. Do ye know the story? Well, it's not one I care to tell, but now—well, now's different.*

  *She'd taken me to town shopping. Not just any town, but Glasgow! Streets crammed with carts and wagons and horses and the new motorcars. So exciting for a young country lad! There was something 'cross the street that I had to go see, though I canna for the life o' me remember what was so important that it made me run, and my mother run after me, right into the path of a car. People rushed*

155

*to her, carried her to the side she'd come from. Through the turning
wheels and legs of the crowd, I saw her white face turn toward me
and smile. She died, Davy. I felt 'twas my fault. If I hadna run—
well. Each night after that, I dreamt of the accident and each night
'twas the same. I could do nothing to help her.*

Gramps, too! I thought

*One day, Davy, I found a sea-rolled flint with a hole in't, like
yers. I showed my friend Meg, who knew things. She said it was a
lucky stone I found. Her Granny called 'em hag stones, fer the hag
that sits on yer stomach at night, paintin' yer dreams with fright. Her
Granny had one hangin' o'er the stable door to keep the devils from
the horses, but Meg said it would work just as well on my own nightmares if I tied it round the bedpost. Meg knew 'bout my dreams, you
see, Davy. So I did what she said, hung the stone from my bedpost,
and had no more dreams of my mother's death. Magic or no, that
foolish stone worked.*

Frances, this Meg must have been like you!

And dreams!

And stones!

Gramps and I have more in common

than I could ever have guessed.

I know what you'd say if you were here:

"Don't be surprised, David.

The pebble

and the mountain

are both made

of rock."

*I kept the stone for a time,* said Gramps, *because it reminded me
of Meg. She moved with her father to London, but before they left,
we took a trip together, the two fathers and Meg and me, to the
Orkney Islands. Now there are some stones ye should see, Davy! Great
standing stones, as tall as two men! Meg found a massive one with a
hole in't and stuck her hand through. "Now you do't, Ali," she said,*

*and we made our promise to each other. I didna' forget. Twelve years later, we married. Meg was yer Gran, Davy.*

*After we married, the stone disappeared. I guess I didna need it then. 'Twas a distinctive stone, much like yers, but for some red marks set into it. It happens sometimes with flint.*

Up my arms,

down my back,

and all around my head,

every hair goes stiff.

I flip the stone,

show Gramps the marks.

His eyebrows frown,

then rise in surprise.

Every part of me waits.

Even the devils in my stomach

float and rest,

and when Gramps answers

the hairs stand taller still.

*If I didna know better,* he whispers,

*I'd say 'twas the very same stone.*

For the hundredth time today, Frances,

I wish you were here

to tell me things,

about the waters underground

that connect ponds and lakes and rivers and oceans.

You'd say it's impossible

for a stone to cross the sea

and work its way inland to me.

You'd say someone dropped it

or some such thing.

But miracles happen, Frances!

I know, because today

for the very first time,

when our fingers met at the stone,
my grandfather's touch
was gentle.

*Davy,* he says. *There's something I need to tell ye. I've had an ill-*
*ness. Ye might have noticed there's less o' me now.*
Laughing, he pats his belly,
and the top of his head.
Beneath brows
thick and white as new snow,
ice-blue eyes twinkle.
I didn't know that inside ice
there could be warmth.

*An illness opens yer eyes, Davy. I know I've been hard on ye, just*
*as I was on yer father before ye. 'Twas the way I was raised by my*
*own dad. But I got thinkin' 'bout baby Bri. I wanted to feel her wee*
*hand curl round my thumb. Do ye know I never held ye as a child?*
*And I only held yer father a few times. 'Twas no a man's place then*
*to be fussin' with a bairn. Once, when yer father was wee, I took him*
*from yer Gran and declared I would change his wet bottom. "Ye'll do*
*no such thing with yer great clumsy hands, Alistair MacDuff!" she*
*said.*
The sound of us laughing together
is a song, Frances.
I'll try to remember the notes
so I can sing it for you.
It's a song worth hearing.

*What I'm tryin' to say, Davy, in my roundabout way is this. I*
*think very well of ye. Yer a fine lad growin' into a fine man. Yer*
*father writes 'bout yer goings on and yer grades at school. He's so*
*proud of ye, Davy. He tells me you still see that lass, Frances. I liked*
*her, Davy, when I met her last time. Heaps o' spirit, just like Meg.*
*I'll say no more, but remember the stone, Davy. The stone works!*

**Sleep**

In darkness I listen
to the snuffles of Bri,
the deep breath of my parents,
the rumbling snore of Gramps.
I cannot see the stone
but know it hangs from my bedpost
and there's not a hag in sight.
I think about you, Frances.
I think about Gramps—
his dream,
the girl he loved,
the stone he found.
Gramps
and stones . . .
Gramps
and stones . . .
This time,
sleep comes
softly as a blanket of black velvet
tucked round a stomach
that's cool and silent
as stone.

# (Kevin)

It's Christmas Eve and I've rounded up my family by the wood stove. My sister, Kate, is curled up on the couch, munching shortbread cookies. It's good to see her eating again. Mom and Dad are squished into the Lazy Boy chair, sharing a bowl of nuts. Spread out on the floor is our bulldog, Kap'n, with two quivering bungee cords of drool stretching floorward from his lips. Katmandu, our Siamese cat, is ignoring the humans as usual. She's in the corner nibbling tinsel off the lower branches of the Christmas tree—a pine this year, my favorite.

"We're ready, Kev," says Mom.

I open the book to where I placed the marker—the red strand of wool from Gaby's scarf—and I begin to read aloud. When they hear what I'm reading, they're surprised. We're not exactly a religious family.

Before this year, I never thought much about angels.

Oh, we have a few (like, a few hundred!) angels around the house at Christmastime. Mom usually goes all out with the decorations, but what can you expect when our family business is a Christmas tree farm? There's the gold angel on the front door wreath and the chorus of wooden cherubs in the kitchen. There's the crumbly Styrofoam-ball angel Kate made in Brownies and the porcelain angels in our crèche.

The year they adopted me and brought me home before Christmas, I was two years old. I don't remember much. But I remember the shiny brown faces of the figures in the crèche. Later Mom told me she painted them that way so I wouldn't feel out of place, being the only one in the house (the only one in town, for that matter) with brown skin.

Whatever the reason, I loved that crèche. Every December, as soon as it came out, I played with the little figures: Mary, Joseph, Jesus, the shepherd boy, the animals, and the three wise guys, as I called them. But I never bothered much with the angels that lounged on the stable roof. They were just ornaments, back-up singers for the main act.

Even up to a couple of months ago, if you asked me what I thought about angels, I would have shrugged and said, "What about them?" But two months ago was before I met Angelica and Gaby, and before Kate got sick. Really sick.

I was in the middle of midterms with essays piling up on the side, when I stormed out of the house one night, belted out a Tarzan yell, a few top-volume yodels and some fairly demonic-sounding Dracula laughs. I was just blowing off steam, but I guess it worried my parents. When I came back inside, they were whispering in the kitchen.

"Kevin?" called Mom.

"Yeah?"

"Come here a minute, will you," said Dad. He always asked

questions like that, without question marks. You couldn't exactly say no.

I poked my head in the kitchen door.

"Are you all right, dear?" asked Mom.

"Yeah. Sorry. It's just . . ." I bugged out my eyes and did my wolfman impression. "Zee moon, she tells me bite off zee head of my math teacher!"

"Why math?" asked Mom.

"We're not zee best of friends tonight, me and my math."

My parents looked at each other and grinned.

"We thought you could use your Christmas present a bit early this year," said Dad. A bit early? It was October. Mom and Dad always turn goofy at Christmas, but this was early even for them.

"What would make life easier for you?" asked Mom.

"Easy. A personal servant with an IQ of 200 who looks just like me and can write these exams. Or a computer."

Mom jumped up and grabbed my hand. "Come! Close your eyes." She dragged me into their bedroom. I could hear Dad opening their closet door.

"*Voilà!*" he said.

I couldn't believe it—box after box of computer stuff! The three of us sat cross-legged on the floor opening everything up.

"A word of warning, though," said Dad. "You have to share this with the rest of us."

"No problem. Kate's going to *flip!*"

A word about Kate. Computers are her life. She can't believe we've lasted this long without one. Kate left for university ten years ago determined to become a doctor. She did, too. But she liked doctoring computers even more than people (they don't talk back, she says), so now she's doing a graduate degree in artificial intelligence.

Even if I wasn't adopted, I'd be wondering why, when they were handing out brains, did Kate get them all? I mean, I thought artificial intelligence was when you tried to pass off a smart friend's homework as your own!

Kate's not just smart either. In her senior year at Lee High, she was president of the student council, captain of the cheerleading team, and she played Queen Elizabeth in the high school's production of the mock royal wedding! Queen Kate is a tough act to follow. First day in a new class is always the same. "So *you* are Kate Kernohan's brother!" the teacher exclaims with respect, and it goes downhill from there.

Kate and I are different as black and white (pun intended). So who could blame me if I hated her? But I can't. No one could. She's great. She sends me postcards with bodacious academic babes on them: "Here's some motivation to help you get through exams. Don't give up! A new life awaits you at university. Love, Kate."

"You'll be able to email her as soon as we get on the Internet," said Dad.

The Internet? *Yesss!*


It wasn't long before I was doing *everything* on the computer—not just homework but surfing the net, meeting people in cyberspace and "talking" to them without getting tongue-tied like I usually do in face-to-face conversations. One night I found a chat box where you can eavesdrop on different conversations until you want to join in. On a channel called Cloud Nine, I ended up talking to people from every corner of the continent. They used handles instead of names. I listened in for a while, then jumped into the conversation, calling myself Komet.


**Hobbes:** So, what is the meaning of life?
**Angelica:** To love and be loved?
**Smitty:** To have a good time, not a long time?
**TNT:** Speak for yourself. Mine's long. Damn long.

Hobbes: Poor lost souls. You're as confused as I am.

Komet: Mind if I pull up a cloud?

TNT: Hey, Komet, seen Haley? Now there's a nice bit of tail!

Komet: Not that kind of Komet. Different one.

Angelica: I think *I* know where you're coming from: On Komet, on Kupid, on Dasher, and Vixen . . . ?

Komet: You guessed it.

Hobbes: Flying reindeer type, eh? Then Komet, *you* must know, if you're supernatural—what's the meaning of life, man?

Komet: Sorry, Santa swore me to secrecy.

We talked like that for a while, just joking around. Smitty and TNT were obviously horny lonely guys, but Hobbes was kind of cool, and Angelica was, well, Angelica was divine. After a while, her name popped up on my screen in a private conversation box. She wanted me, just me!

Angelica: So, Komet, do you really believe in Santa Claus?

Komet: I have to. He's the one who feeds me carrots and hot fudge sundaes.

Angelica: *Hot* fudge? At the North Pole?

Komet: Modern technology. Microwaves!

Angelica: :-) Well, if you believe in Santa, let me ask you this: Do you also believe in angels?

Komet: Hmm . . . a flying life form like myself. I've never seen one, but that doesn't mean they don't exist.

Angelica: Hold onto your hot fudge, Komet. They do exist!

Komet: How do you know? Are *you* an angel?

Angelica: I am, if you believe I am.

I almost did believe her. Why not? It was almost harder to believe I could log on to my computer and find a real flesh-and-blood girl who was so easy to talk to. For once I wasn't a blithering idiot talking to a girl. I was suave slick Komet. I was Cyberguy, the Net Hunk.

I could picture Angelica in my mind, a beautiful Whitney Houston face to match that beautiful voice on the screen. But the longer we talked, the more I had to know for sure what she looked like.

> **Angelica:** Well, if you *must* know. I'm six feet tall with hairy pecs so strong you could crack an egg on them.
> **Komet:** If you're a hairy male, then I'm the Queen of England.
> **Angelica:** Okay, okay. I'm five foot two, eyes of blue . . . and 82!
> **Komet:** Too bad. I'm only 75, and I make it a policy never to flirt with older women.
> **Angelica:** :-) Okay, the truth. But you go first.
> **Komet:** Four legs, fur coat, big lips, overbite, antlers . . .
> **Angelica:** Ah, yes, my fellow flyer, and I'm the angel. Wings, halo, sweetness and light. I wonder, would you even know me if you saw me?

She was right. I mean, this girl could be twenty or thirty or fifty years old! She could have total facial disfigurement! She could be married! She could be a he! But I was never so comfortable talking to anyone before.

I found out that she lived in Toronto. She didn't have a chance to ask where I lived. All of a sudden, she wrote "Oops! Gotta log off!"

"Don't go!" I wrote. "There's so much I don't know. What do

you eat for breakfast? What do you like to read? What do you dream about at night?" But she was gone.

"Still up, Kev?" yawned Mom, sticking her head around the corner. "How's the project coming?" I was supposed to be finishing a presentation for English class. We had to speak on the theme of Christmas, and I was doing my speech on—what else?—Christmas trees. I wasn't worried about it. I've given enough tours that I know it all by heart, and I'm not so nervous speaking about things I know well.

"Fine, Mom. Just pulling some stuff off the net."

"Well, don't stay up all night. Your Dad and I are heading to bed."

"'Night, Mom." She closed the door, and I stared at the screen, wondering how to find an angel that has disappeared.

The next afternoon, I managed to stay awake long enough to give my speech and answer questions at the end. People always ask about the K's. Our Christmas tree farm is called Kernohan's Kristmas Trees. We're all K's in my family, except for my father, Harold (but at Christmas time we call him "Hark", as in "Hark the Herald"). The K's started with my mother, Kathryn. Then Kate was born, and they adopted me, Kevin. We got a bulldog along the way, Kaptain Kirk, and a Siamese cat named Katmandu. Part of our business is a petting zoo that we sometimes take to country fairs and shopping malls during the off-season. Like a modern-day Noah's ark, our zoo has his-and-her pairs of animals: Kisser and Kasper, the geese; Kandy and Kingsley, the pigs; Karlotta and Konrad, the sheep, and so on. The class thought it was hilarious.

There was a new girl in class that day who had just moved from Toronto. She had city written all over her—platform-soled, lace-up boots, a velvet mini skirt and a tie-dye T-shirt under her open leather jacket that, from what I could see, read:

*f y*
*lie*
*ge*

The hair around her face was long, blonde and curly, but from her ears back, it was shaved close to her head and dyed red. Her skin was pale and painted with heavy black eyeliner and lipstick. The right side of her nose was pierced, and a little red jewel nestled there.

I tried not to stare, but how could I help it? She smiled at me. Hey, I thought, maybe I really *am* Cyberguy, the Net Hunk! Or maybe, since I was the only non-Caucasian in the entire class, she was just acknowledging the other person who looked different. I wished I had the nerve to speak to her, but what would I say? *Uh, do you know a girl named Angelica who lives in Toronto, too? I think I'm in love with her.*

My speech was second-to-last, and Mitch Tyne finished up with a talk about Christmas desserts. During the speech, the new girl passed me a note: "Great speech! Kool business! But aren't you koncerned that you're kommercializing Kristmas? Gaby."

I tried to write back. I wrote a couple of sentences using K words, but it came out sounding stupid. The suave devil Komet was back home in the computer. I crumpled up the paper and tossed it into my knapsack.

Mitch wound up her speech by passing around sample desserts (food means an automatic A from Mr. Miller). We were stuffing our faces when the new girl raised her hand and said, "Should I give my speech today?"

Surely Mr. Miller didn't expect her to give a speech, unprepared, on her very first day. And was she some kind of psycho to volunteer? Mr. Miller looked as surprised as the rest of us. He brushed the cookie crumbs from his moustache and said, "It's not necessary, Gaby, but you're welcome to, of course. Did you have a topic in mind?"

"Has anyone talked about angels yet?"

*What's with angels,* I wondered. *Is Someone trying to tell me something?* I pinched myself, and it hurt, so I figured I wasn't dead yet. Then I realized that if this new girl knew about angels, maybe she knew Angelica! Maybe they had an Angel Club in Toronto or something.

But when Gaby started speaking, I lost my train of thought. Her voice sort of reached out like a hand, picked me up and carried me away. She didn't use notes, but she never stumbled over her words. They poured out of her like music.

Angels, she said, are everywhere. They're our messengers, teachers and muses. From the moment we're born, a guardian angel watches over us. When you hear a voice inside you, guiding you, that's your angel. When you feel *déjà vu,* your angel is giving you a memory to show you the way. And then she told the Christmas story. The way Gaby told it, you could actually see the stars over Bethlehem, hear the pounding of the angels' wings as they descended from heaven and smell the warm animal scents of the manger. Never again would I ignore those angels in our crèche. Gaby brought them to life for me.

At the end of her speech, Gaby paused and held open her black leather jacket. I read the message—the *whole* message— along with everyone else in the class: SMILE if you believe in angels! And you know, I don't think there was a single person who wasn't smiling.


That night, I was reading Kate's email message just as Mom's phone rang downstairs.

Kev, got some bad news. Need some tests at the hospital. I'm sure it's nothing. Don't let Mom worry. Means I'll miss the big season opener, though. You'll have to wear Kerny for me! Oh, quit groaning! You have good legs. It's about time you showed them off in stockings.

Love, Kate :-)

Kerny is our farm's mascot. Kate usually wears the costume during the Christmas tree season. She's a natural with the kids and doesn't mind looking stupid. The costume is a green fuzzy Christmas tree that makes your hips look about five feet wide. You wear a star on top of your head, leggings striped like candy canes and shiny red boots on your feet. There are colored ornaments pinned all over it that jingle when you walk. Kate usually strolls around the main yard belting out Christmas carols and handing out candy canes to the kiddies.

Mom came upstairs looking worried.

"Kev? That was Kate."

"Yeah, she just emailed me."

"Oh? Did she tell you about the tests?"

"She said it's probably nothing."

"I hope so, but she said there's a lump under one arm. I'm worried."

"If Kate said she'll be okay, I'm sure she will be. When has Kate ever been wrong about anything?" I gave Mom a bear hug, and Kaptain Kirk parked himself between our legs.

"See?" I said. "Kap'n doesn't want you to worry either."

But a *lump!* I didn't like the sound of that. After Mom left, I tried to find Angelica. I had so much to tell her about Kate and Gaby's speech, but she wasn't on Cloud Nine or in any other chat room, not that night or any night after that. I never found her again. It was as if she had vanished into thin air. Soon after, Kate was diagnosed with Hodgkin's disease, and Mom left right away to be with her. Cancer.

*Angel, my angel,* I wondered, *where are you now?*

Kate and Mom came home together, with Kate trying as usual to cheer everyone up in spite of the fact that she looked awful. Dad hugged her.

"How are you, Kate," he said.

"Fine, Dad."

When I hugged her, it was like hugging someone else, and for a minute I got scared, as if the real Kate was already gone. "Kate, you're so skinny!"

"Such a charmer, this guy. Knows just what to say to the ladies."

She was right. What a jerk. "I'm sorry."

She swatted my head. "It's okay. With Mom's good cooking, I'm bound to gain weight." She looked from me to Dad to Mom again.

"Knock it off, you guys! Don't look so tragic! This is a curable cancer. But you still have to wear Kerny, Kev, no matter how much you hate it."

I didn't feel like wearing Kerny. I didn't feel like doing anything. Suddenly the whole crazy way we do Christmas seemed so crass and tasteless. All the "K's" were giving me a headache. I wanted Christmas to be like Gaby had described it, special and simple, with the stars clear and bright overhead, the soft murmur of sleeping animals and the warm scent of hay wrapped round it all.

A parade of Kate's friends trooped through to visit. Most of them I never knew, but I got to know Kate's best friend, Jewel, around the time of the mock royal wedding. Jewel was Princess Diana, and I was one of her page boys. The three of us took down the "official portrait" that Mom has hanging in the dining room. It actually looks quite authentic, except for me, the lone dash of color in the otherwise Caucasian front row. It never bothered me before. But everything bothered me now.

Kate and Jewel were busy talking about Alex Meyers, their friend who played the part of Princess Anne. Alex died when they were still in high school. No one said it, but I bet we were all thinking the same thing: *Is Kate the next to go?*

I pulled on my coat and slammed outside. I scooped up some snow and held it against my burning cheeks. Suddenly Kate was beside me, pulling up her jacket around her ears.

"Kev . . . I'm going to beat this thing. I believe that. You have to believe it too, okay? I need you to."

*I am, if you believe I am.*

"I believe it, Kate."

"Good."

Then we threw back our heads and howled at the stars.

I was wearing Kerny, striped stockings and all, when Gaby arrived at the farm, looking cuter than ever in a bright red parka. She introduced me to her older brother, Ross, his wife, Tracey, and her niece, Quenby, who looked like a mini Gaby without the makeup and wild hairdo. I gave them each a candy cane.

"How's your holiday going?" I asked.

"Pretty good, but it never seems long enough, you know?"

"Tell me about it. It's hard to go Christmas shopping when you're stuck wearing a tree all day. I can hardly fit through the door at the mall."

Gaby laughed at my lame joke, thank goodness. I've learned that it's better to make jokes about yourself than wait for other people to do it.

"Gaby gets to choose the twee," said Quenby.

"Ah!" I waved my mittened hand toward the fields. "Take your pick. What kind of a person are you? Spruce? Pine? Fir?"

"I don't know," said Gaby, "but I'll know the right one when I see it."

I showed them where to get a saw and where to catch the wagon that would take them out to the fields. I wondered why she was here with her brother's family. Did she live with them? I kept watching for her, but it was a full two hours before they returned, empty-handed.

"I just didn't see the perfect tree," Gaby sighed.

"*I* saw yots of twees *I* yiked," grumbled Quenby, who was peeking in my basket for another candy cane.

Gaby's brother and sister-in-law looked freezing cold and ready to throw Gaby into the nearest snowbank.

"Let me get you something warm from the Snack Shack," I said.

Quenby, Ross and Tracey sat at the picnic bench to have their hot chocolate, but since I couldn't sit down in my costume very well, Gaby and I leaned against the side of the shack. We watched the people coming and going with their kids on sleighs, dragging trees, having a great time. She was easy to talk to and didn't once make me feel stupid for wearing a fuzzy Christmas tree costume.

"Your farm isn't what I expected," she said. "I love how you turn a corner and find a statue of a gnome or a deer. It's like getting lost in an enchanted forest, except there aren't any dragons."

I thought of Kate's cancer. Maybe, through a microscope, that's exactly what it looked like. A dragon.

"Your family sure must love Christmas," said Gaby.

"Yeah, Mom especially goes nuts this time of year." But so far Mom had done no baking, no decorating inside the house. Like me, she just wasn't in the mood.

"So you live with your brother?" I asked.

Gaby didn't speak for a moment. "For now. My parents are in the city. . . . You're lucky, Kevin, to have such a great family."

"I guess I am."

"You're adopted, eh?"

"How did you know?"

"I'm adopted, too," she said.

"You *are*? But Quenby could be your kid sister, she looks so much like you."

"Coincidence. We're not blood relatives."

"Oh. . . . They seem nice, though, your brother's family."

"They put up with me. If my parents were here, they'd freak out, say forget about getting a tree, squeal off in a huff and hold it against me for the rest of my life what a miserable day they had. You won the lottery getting your family, Kevin. . . . Here, hold this."

She gave me her hot chocolate and squatted down to check out the tree that was lying behind the shack. It was no good. There was a big hole in one side and a forked top. A real Charlie Brown Christmas tree. I don't even know where it came from. Dad's usually a stickler for keeping the trees pruned.

Gaby hauled the tree upright and leaned it against the wall.

"Why was it just lying there?"

"It's garbage. We'll probably cut it up for firewood."

"No, you won't! This is our Christmas tree."

"*This* tree?"

"Yes. It needs a good home."

I gave it to her, of course, on the house. Her brother took one look at it and shook his head, but he didn't look surprised. It was late in the afternoon and getting dark. Ross and Tracey tied the tree to the roof of their car. They got Quenby buckled in and climbed in, too.

Time to say good-bye. Last time I said good-bye to a girl I liked, I never heard from her again. And this time, not only did I forget all the brilliant things I was going to say, I was wearing a dorky costume with striped stockings.

But Gaby planted a kiss on my cheek that was as warm as a roasted marshmallow. "Thank-you Kevin," she whispered. "And don't worry about your sister. She's going to be okay. I just know it."

"My sister?" I didn't remember mentioning Kate's cancer, although I *had* been thinking about it. It was always on my mind.

Gaby climbed into the back seat and rolled down the window. Her breath puffed out to me in a sweet peppermint breeze.

"I've been off the Net for a while," she said, "what with the move and all, but Ross is hooking us up this week. Would you join me on Cloud Nine some time? Maybe we could pick up where we left off."

Before I could say a word, before it even sank in that she was my vanished angel, the car pulled away. At my feet was a strand of soft red wool from her scarf. I picked it up and wrapped it around my finger, the way Kate does when she has something important to remember.

They're enjoying the story, I can tell. Mom's got that mushy look in her eyes that means we've started a new Christmas tradition. The room is warm and filled with the scent of hay from the display that Mom set up this afternoon ("Better late than never!" she said). At Kate's feet, Kap'n and Katmandu are curled up together in a noisy hairy tangle of bulldog snores and cat purrs. Not quite a Bethlehem stable on the night a miracle happened, but close enough for me. I've reached the part in the story when the angels appear to the shepherds in a great flash of light, and it's Gaby's voice that I hear in my head, saying the words along with me: "Fear not: for, behold, I bring you tidings of great joy. . . ."

1999

# (Ginger)

Finally here. The old Lee Cemetery. Just a two-hour drive but, God, it seemed to take forever. Like going through one of those slo-mo time-warp scenes where the voices echo.

*You-oo are-r now-ow entering-ing your-or past-ast-ast. . . .*

Had to come through the main gate. The one I used before is padlocked with a sign saying, *Plot owners use highway entrance. All others respect these sacred grounds.*

Wonder if they found out what I used to do here? Maybe others did it, too. I meant no disrespect. I was looking for respect. Or love, anyway.

Other than the welcome sign, place looks the same as I remember. Hilly, wild . . . *unkempt.* That's what Miss Twitchit used to say: "Ginger, you are looking decidedly *unkempt* today."

I park beside the caretaker's cottage. Used to think elves lived there. Almost begged old George, the caretaker, if I could live there, too. Keep an eye on things for him. Keep things tidy. But I never got up the nerve to ask him. He knew who I was, though. Saw me here all the time, up the highest hill, sitting under the pines. He'd wave and slur, "G'day miss" through yellow teeth.

Always chewing tobacco, George was. He was a nice man. A good man.

Groan from Jo. She always hates to leave her dreams, but the minute her eyes are open, she starts bouncing around like Silly Putty on a trampoline. How she does it, I haven't a clue. Takes *me* half an hour and a couple of coffees to wake up proper. Wonder what she'll say when she sees where I've brought her? Always full of questions, Jo is. Why? Why? Why? 'Course, some days, I ask myself the same thing.

"Jo, love?"

"Mmm?"

"We're here."

"Where?" she yawns.

"Lee Cemetery. Used to live down the road when I was a kid."

In that stinking hole of a house with carpets reeking of cat pee and Albert's sour booze breath landing heavy as a slap on my ear. A crowded house with four cats and Lil's giant pear of a body and Albert's oily fingers always on the move—rubbing Lil's full moon butt or the skin on my upper arms. Get goose bumps now just thinking about it.

"Never really thought of that house as home, though," I tell Jo. "Used to spend most of my time here."

She gives me that Mom-you-are-sooo-weird look, jumps out of the car and looks around.

"This place is cool," she says. Phew, she likes it. Guess Jo's the unkempt type, too. Wonder if she was born like that or if it rubbed off from me? Tish says we're not born, we're made. She's done a whack of films, weird arty stuff about that very thing, about how the fairy tales we learn as kids make us act a certain way later on. Me, I'm not sure. Thought I hated those corny Disney movies; then I had a kid and fell in love with them all over again. Cinderella, Sleeping Beauty, Snow White . . . Next thing I knew I had a seven-year-old Spice Girl doing sexy dance moves and singing, "Do you wanna be my lover?" Did I make her that way, I wonder? Did Disney?

At least today she's ditching the sexpot attitude to be my fellow adventurer, here in my old stomping ground. Jo runs ahead to the little white pioneer stones. I poke along behind, still feeling like I'm half here, half somewhere else. . . .

Man, I love these stones. Comforting as a mug of hot chocolate on a rainy day. Maybe 'cause they're so old, older than people, older than dinosaurs. Sure they're headstones now, but that's just temporary. Look at the pioneer stones. Already you can hardly read them. Worn down by rain and fuzzed over with lichen, they're slipping back in the ground.

Farther in, I see more changes. Hills that were bare when I was a kid are now covered with gravestones. I get an awful feeling that maybe all the people I knew in Lee are dead, even the ones my age. Like there's Les Fletcher. Nice guy, kind of a party animal, played hockey with Derek. According to this he died two years ago. Man. And, of course, Alex Meyers is buried here. She died when we were still in high school. The first to go.

Jo's stopped at a stone I always loved, pink granite with a little stone castle carved on top. *Sweet Dreams, Our Darling Infant Girls.* Like a fist in the gut, I feel grief for those poor dead babies. This grave never bothered me before, but it means something different to me now, now that I have Jo.

I rest on the stone bench by Alma Harper's grave with the half circle of cedars curving round me. They've grown tall, and pale green ivy's growing up them. I hunker down to look under the bench. Somewhere are my initials. Here. I trace them with my finger. What was I—twelve?—when I scratched them into the stone? And below mine are Derek's, carved by me five years later, where no one would see them. That was long after the end. The *end.* Ain't that a joke.

"Hey, Mom. Race you to the top!"

Didn't take Jo long to find the best spot in the cemetery, my old place at the top of the hill where two pine trees grow so close together, their roots and branches are tangled up. I used to sit between their trunks and pretend they were my grandparents, an old man and woman hugging overhead.

Huffing and puffing, I follow Jo up. You can see the whole township from the top of this hill. Used to pretend I was queen, and my subjects lived down in the town. Had the hill to myself then, but they've sold some plots up here now. Petrie. Phillips. Marchand. Don't recognize the names. I turn my back to them and sit under the pines.

"Isn't it pretty, Jo?"

"Yup." She barely glances at the view. What's she looking at on the ground? Two beetles, crawling over each other. Please don't let them be mating. I can't answer those questions today.

"Look at these guys wrasslin', Mom!"

"That's right, Jo," I laugh. "wrasslin'."

And suddenly I'm no longer half here. I'm all *there,* back then. Eighteen years younger. Eighty pounds lighter.

Wrasslin'. Wrasslin'.


I can't stop the shaking in my hands. Even when I pound them against the wall and slap them against my cheeks, they keep shaking. Can't stop the goddamned sobs either, that flap like bats against my insides, then rise and rip out my throat.

"You must a set 'er off some'ow!" Lil hisses outside my door.

"Wassn't me!" That's Albert. Six-foot-one but he can whine like a two-year-old. "She come home from school that way. Try to be nice, she calls me names and shuts herself up in there! Well screw her!"

Lil sighs. "Bert, make yourself useful and put on the tea."

"House full of bossy bitches," he grumbles, but then I hear Lil giggle, and I know he's tickling her, buttering her up. Traitor Lil.

Two sharp knocks. "Come on, luv, open up!"

She rattles the handle. I've dragged my dresser in front of the door.

"Ginger? Fine, don't answer then, but I'm only here for a bite. Workin' evenin' shift at the drugstore. Be home by 9:30. Bert's here if you need him, 'kay?"

*Need* him? He'd love that.

"And eat somethin', will you? You're wasting away."

The cemetery. Have to get to the cemetery without them seeing me. Quiet as I can, I pry out the screen and climb through the window. It's a tight squeeze, even for me, but I make it. Almost land on top of Tiger, who's pissing in the garden. I go round the back of the house so Albert won't see me and cut through the neighbor's yard to the road. Then I sprint. The air's like a waterfall crashing over my face and through my hair, so by the time I reach the cemetery, I almost feel clean.

The sobs start again as I run to the top of my hill. It's dusk. No one else is here. This place is mine. Home. And to think I almost wrecked it. I curl into a ball, put my head between my knees, try to block out the voices in my ears. It's no use.

"*I give you this place.*" Giggling, nervous. That was me, to Derek. I was wild about him. He was crazy about me, too. I know he was. He looked right into me and saw me, not like everyone else who'd look through me as if I wasn't there. Used to call me every night and give me little presents all the time. I didn't have any money. What could I give him? So I brought him here, to my special place.

He kissed me, touched my hair. "Weirdo."

*Weirdo?* Oh God, I did the wrong thing. Said the wrong thing. Again.

"Ginger, I'm just kidding! This place is great. At least we can be alone."

Wouldn't take Derek to my house, not with the pee smell and

Albert there, out of work, hanging around. Derek's house was full of brothers and hockey equipment. Front hall jammed with skates, pads, jocks and socks drying out. His mom didn't care. She was nuts about hockey, too, maybe even more than the boys. She knew Derek would be a star. And she knew I'd never last. Told me so with her eyes: I wasn't right for him. Foster kid. Too poor.

Voices. *I love you. I love you, Ginger.* That was Derek, sometime later, after we'd come here a lot. We found a private place near the trees where we'd lie down and kiss. Didn't need a blanket. The grass was our blanket. The leaves were our blanket. Stones and sticks and hard bumpy ground melted away when I was with Derek. Felt nothing but him. Nothing but good.

The ring. Same ring that's pinching the life out of my pinky finger right now. Found its way from Derek's mouth to mine while kissing. Couldn't believe it. A ring! Real diamonds, too. Tiny, but real! Tried to put it on my right hand, but he said no, this one, and slipped it on my wedding finger. Stared deep into me, said some words we learned in English class: "With this ring, I pledge thee my troth." In class we'd laughed along with everyone else, but winked at each other when no one was looking. And in the private place by the trees, on the cold October ground, we didn't laugh. I wanted to cry, I loved him so much.

Voices. *What's wrong, Derek? Is it me?* Me. Pathetic. Losing him, not knowing why or how to stop it. Willing to do anything. Anything. Because we hadn't done everything, though I'd wanted to, felt ready to. Things speeded up without me. Hockey. Derek the star. No one could catch him. Groupies, niners, hung out at the rink. His mom would hug him, ignore me. Older guys would buy him beer, take him to parties I never heard about till after.

One day Derek didn't show up for class and neither did Molly Freestone, one of the carbon copy cheerleaders, and the next day he broke up with me. Molly didn't last long, but I knew he had sex with her. She'd have sex with anyone. There were others after her. Lots of others. By graduation I bet Derek had slept with the whole cheerleading team.

Voices. *Don't worry your head over puppy luv, Ginger. There's plenty o' fish in the sea.* Lil, dishing out one of her clichés to make me feel better. Didn't work, but I did take her advice. Two can play that game, I said to myself in the spring. Matched Derek, conquest by conquest. Derek got a new girl; I got a new guy. Not that I was great looking. Red hair, kind of skinny. But the guys seemed to like the way I fed their egos. It was easy. Just tell them how gorgeous they were, how wonderful they made me feel, how I never felt this good before. Just a matter of acting.

Took the guys to the cemetery, my spot by the trees. And what I didn't do with Derek, I'd do with them. Got easy after a while. Suck back a few brew, let the numbness flow in, lay back, make the right sounds, pretend. It was dark by the trees. I could blot out the face over me so it was just a black hole against the stars. Then I could put anyone's face there, and sometimes it was a face with blue eyes and black hair. Derek's.

Voices. Two guys by the water fountain at school. Both guys that I'd taken to the cemetery. Cute guys, nice guys, or so I thought. They were laughing, swatting each other's backs. Then I heard it.

*. . . with the 'Graveyard Girl.'*
*No way! He did her, too?*

They were talking about me. I know, 'cause when they saw me standing there, they shut right up. I couldn't think of one thing to say, no couldn't-care-less, you-guys're-letting-your-tongues-wag-as-much-as-your-dicks kind of comebacks.

Something snapped. I think it was me. Like the rubber bands I used to wind around my thumb till the tip turned purple. Like I'd squeezed all my feelings into my thumb and then—*poing!* Ran to the bathroom. Flushed the toilet over and over till I got the crying under control. Cut my last class and ran home. Should have gone straight to the cemetery, but I held back. Kept hearing the voices. *Graveyard Girl.*

Voices. Albert's now. Slurred. *Why don't you give me a little of that?*

*A little of what?*

*You know.* Stinking booze breath pinned me to the wall, fingers soft and rubbery as hot dogs gliding up and down my arms.

*Get away from me!*

*You're upset. Come sit on my knee. I'll make it better.*

Shoved him back. Yelled something, can't remember what, but it made him mad. Chased me through the living room. Down the hall. Lucky I was light and fast. Lucky he was drunk and slow. Made it to my room, slammed the door, dragged the dresser in front of it.

*Stay away!*

*Thump, thump, thump* on the door. *Come on, honey.*

*I'll tell Lil!*

*You'll tell her nothin' cause nothin' happened! Fine, stay in there an' cool off awhile. Jesus! I was just tryin' to be nice.*

*Go away, or . . .*

*I'm goin'. I'm goin'.*

*. . . or I'll kill you.*

Whispered that so faint, I could hardly hear it. Could hardly believe I said it. Said it and meant it.

Voices. *Ginger, do you ever wish you could rewind, erase your memories, and start over?* That was Tish. First real girl friend I ever had. Took me long enough. Tish wasn't a giggler, like most of the other girls. She was quiet, big boned with short brown hair and brown eyes. People said she was a dyke. Drew some stares when we started hanging out.

Tish was Alex Meyer's friend before Alex got in with the cheerleading crowd. We had pretty much the same opinion of cheerleaders. Tish was in my Family Studies class. Got to talking about videos one day, and she said that thing about rewinding and erasing, and I said, "That's the first *real* thing anyone's said to me in a long time." And Tish knew what I meant.

After that, I hung out at her house a lot. Her Baba was sick with Alzheimer's, and Tish had to watch her after school till her mom got home from work. I liked it there. It was peaceful. No one to run away from.

After what I heard at the water fountain, Tish was the only person I took to the cemetery. She used to go there anyway to sit by Alex's grave. We'd sit at the top of the hill and talk. Sometimes we'd take our cameras and shoot some film. Took a whole series called The Graveyard Girls. Figured out the personalities of the different stones, dressed them up with hats and scarves, and took their pictures. This tall curvy one here with the bowling ball head we dressed up as Marilyn Monroe, red lipstick and all. Meant no disrespect. Cleaned it up afterward.

Dress up. A game you don't outgrow. Jo was into it awhile back, prancing around all day in a cardboard crown, pretending to be that real princess, Fergie's kid—what's her name? Oh yeah, Eugenie. Jo wouldn't have even known about her if it wasn't for her Diana-obsessed kindergarten teacher. What a case that chick was. A real mini Miss Twitchit. Usually when your kid starts school you worry about them picking up things like chicken pox and head lice, but Jo wound up lovesick with a big fat crush on Diana's kid, Prince William. Oh she had it bad. Drew a bunch of pictures for him and begged me to mail them to his "castle." Must've thought he'd call her up and invite her to a ball! My poor little Cinderella Jo, stuck here in Canada.

Maybe I should show her the picture I ripped out of my yearbook and stuffed into my pocket this morning. The photo I took myself of the mock royal wedding they put on at the high school. The Wedding of the Century! The Greatest Show on Earth! Our chance to be part of history! Except it was fake.

I aimed the camera that day at all those fake princes and

princesses, all those people who laughed behind my back and called me Graveyard Girl, all those people who treated Derek like he really was a prince, better than the rest of us. I aimed and pressed the shutter release. Felt like I was pulling a trigger. A firing squad of one.

I won't tell Jo that part. But maybe if I show her the picture, she'll see how dumb they look, big kids dressed up, pretending to be something they weren't. Or maybe she'd think they look great. She's still a kid after all. Still a dreamer.

On the way up here, we heard on the radio about the other royal wedding. Prince Edward's marrying a girl named Sophie today. A Diana look alike, except I guess she's older and wiser.

Jo was wild. "A *real* wedding, with a *real* prince!? Why didn't you tell me?"

"I didn't know honey. I'm sorry." Not completely true. Guess I'd heard something about it, but they didn't make as big a news splash about this royal wedding as they did with the others. Must've heard something about it though. Maybe that's what got me thinking about things today.

"We'll see it on the news tonight," I said. If we can pry your dad away from the TV. Tonight's the final game of the Stanley Cup playoffs, and whether I like it or not, we'll be celebrating my birthday munching chips and dip off the ottoman.

For now Jo seems to have forgotten about the wedding. Maybe later I'll take her to the pub in town for lunch. They're sure to be showing the wedding on TV. Maybe Miss Twitchit will be there, sipping sherry and waving a Union Jack.

"If I lie down," says Jo, "do you think I could roll all the way to the bottom?"

Normally I say things like "be careful" and "don't get dirty." But today I say, "You never know till you try, Jo. Go ahead."

"Okay. You watch!"

She's beautiful, Jo is. Looks like Ray with sandy brown hair and huge grey eyes. There was a time I thought about kids with black hair and blue eyes. Kids that could skate like the wind.

I dig the newspaper clipping out of my pocket. The date at the top is today's date, June 19, 1999. *Papp Weds Atlanta Beauty.* The clipping shows a picture of Derek and his new wife, a pretty blonde, posing in their wedding outfits in front of a goal net. Both of them are wearing skates. Apparently she plays hockey, too. They got married right after the Leafs' last game of the series. Derek's just signed on with the new Atlanta team, the Thrashers, which'll mean fewer appearances in my living room. Ray never misses *Hockey Night in Canada,* and Derek Papp has always been one of his favorite Maple Leafs.

One night, Ray was reading the paper while I brushed out Jo's hair. "Hey, Ginge, says here that Derek Papp comes from Lee, too. How come you never told me? Did you know him?"

"Papp?" I said, real casual. "Yeah, I knew him, sort of. Everyone did."

"Mom! Did you see that?" Jo yells from the bottom of the hill, snaps me back to the present. I'm losing that time-warp feeling. The inside of my head is quiet. No more voices.

"Yup, you're a real rock 'n' roller!"

She laughs. "Your turn!"

"Not that way!" I yell back. "I'll be down in just a sec."

There's something I've come to do today. With a stick, I dig a hole the size of a hockey puck between the pine trees. I twist off the ring and drop it into the hole along with the balled-up clipping and the picture from my yearbook. I flick some dirt over it and whisper, "Ashes to ashes, dust to dust." I push the rest of the dirt back in the hole, stomp it with my foot and scatter pine needles over top.

Then I holler after Jo, "Look out, baby, here I come!" and run like stink down the hill with nothing weighing me down, not the eighteen years or the eighty pounds or even the throbbing in my pinky finger.

RICHARD EASTMAN

*wendy* a. *lewis* has been a tutor, retail store owner, marketing representative, public relations consultant and, most recently, a writer. She studied literature at the University of Toronto and currently resides in Uxbridge, Ontario. *Graveyard Girl* is her first collection of stories for teens.